All Tied Up

Pleasure Inn, Book 1

Need the job done right? Get a handyman with the right...*tools*.

Interior decorator Lindsay Bell jumped at the chance to help restore the old inn at Mason Creek. What could be more fun than letting her imagination run wild on an unlimited budget? Eagerly she plans to turn her assigned room into a fantasy BDSM playground.

All she expected from her newly hired handyman was to help her tear down a support wall. She certainly didn't expect Brad Caldwell to be so drop-dead gorgeous in a tool belt. When he proves to be a steady, hardworking, stand-up guy—unlike the men she's dated—Lindsay has a new and wicked idea.

To take her new creation on a test drive down the road of their deepest, darkest, most delicious desires—and seduce her way into his heart.

Warning: Smokin' hot sex with creative use of toys, and a dash of magic.

All Worked Up

Pleasure Inn, Book 2

It's just one little bet. Winner takes...*all.*

Tired of aspiring actors using her to get close to her movie-producer father, Candace Steele has sworn off relationships. At least until she's achieved her dream of restoring an old inn on the outskirts of Mason Creek. The new carpenter who's been hired to help her create bedroom furniture designed for...endurance...is throwing a kink into her plans. Watching his athletic body pound wood is doing things to her hormones that have her rethinking her vow.

When he agreed to take the job, Marc Collins intended to keep the sexy spitfire at arm's length. But Candace is giving him a run for his money in more ways than one. It's tough to keep just his eyes on—and hands off—his boss's daughter when she's hell-bent on seducing him. And when she pulls a fast one and wins an impromptu bet, what's a red-blooded guy to do except let her collect her winnings...all of them.

The heat they generate melts the fresh paint off the walls. But when seeds of doubt make Candace put on her running shoes to flee, Marc will have to talk fast—and run faster—to capture her heart.

Warning: This red-hot story contains graphic sex, frank language, wet play, use of orgasm-enhancing props, and to top it all off, it's all caught on film—just in case you missed anything the first time.

All Lit Up

Pleasure Inn, Book 3

Rebuilding the fire—one kiss at a time.

When interior designer Anna Deveau is hired to create a room made for romance at a Victorian inn, she is thrilled—and a little wistful. A fairy-tale ending will never be hers, but perhaps tapping into abandoned dreams will fan the flames for someone else.

Then she learns the only bricklayer available to build the room's fireplace is Daniel Long. The sexy boy-next-door who filled her teen years with angst, broke her heart—and still colors her nights with red-hot fantasies.

Daniel never understood why Anna stopped talking to him a week before her sweet-sixteen party. Or why the wall between them remains a mile high. But now that he's back in town, he intends to figure it out once and for all. Pushing the limits of her seductive design, he sets out to prove he didn't burn her in the past.

Anna finds herself doing the one thing she swore she'd never do again: laying herself bare. Until the ghost of rumors past threatens to snuff out the fiery fantasy that, this time, Anna thought was real...

Warning: Years of sinful fantasies about the sexy boy-next-door lead to a night of wild indulgence. Be sure to keep a bevy of toys on hand when reading this tale, or better yet, get a boy-next-door of your own.

Look for these titles by
Cathryn Fox

Now Available:

Blood Ties
One on One
Dance of the Dragon

Print Anthology
Claimed

Pleasure Inn

Cathryn Fox

SAMHAIN
PUBLISHING

Samhain Publishing, Ltd.
577 Mulberry Street, Suite 1520
Macon, GA 31201
www.samhainpublishing.com

Pleasure Inn
Print ISBN: 978-1-60928-017-8
All Tied Up Copyright © 2011 by Cathryn Fox
All Worked Up Copyright © 2011 by Cathryn Fox
All Lit Up Copyright © 2011 by Cathryn Fox

Editing by Anne Scott
Cover by Scott Carpenter

All Tied Up, ISBN 978-1-60504-530-6
First Samhain Publishing, Ltd. electronic publication: May 2009
All Worked Up, ISBN 978-1-60504-842-0
First Samhain Publishing, Ltd. electronic publication: December 2009
All Lit Up, ISBN 978-1-60504-969-4
First Samhain Publishing, Ltd. electronic publication: March 2010
First Samhain Publishing, Ltd. print publication: March 2011

Contents

All Tied Up

Dedication

To Mark, with much love.

Prologue

"Just because we've all sworn off men, certainly doesn't mean we have to lock down the candy shop, girls."

Summoned by those forlorn words, Pamina, Goddess of Passion and Everything Enchanted, put down her paperback and lifted her long lithe frame from her cozy recliner. With unhurried steps, she padded barefoot to her bay window and peered out. She brushed her golden hair from her shoulders and pulled the morning air into her lungs. The scent of lilac carried in on the breeze and curled around her. A smile touched her mouth as two lovebirds frolicked on the perch of her bird feeder. Ah, such a beautiful autumn day, she mused.

The perfect season for lovers.

Sunlight burst through the clouds and glistened off the crisp red apples weighing down the branches on her fruit tree. Her cat Abracadabra jumped onto the window ledge beside her, curled himself into a ball and lazily groomed himself.

"I guess it's that time again, Abra." She gathered all twenty-five pounds of fur ball into her arms and gave him a knowing wink. As the Goddess of Passion, when a woman, or in this case, three women, uttered the dismal words "sworn off men", it meant she had work to do. It was time for her to summon a bit of magic, spread a little passion and show these women they were far too young to rely on sex toys for the rest of their lives. Their perfect match was still out there, just waiting to be found, with a little help from her, of course.

Abra huffed, and in that squeaky little cat voice of his said, "Well, it's about time." Restless, he pounced back onto the sill. Mystical eyes sparkled with interest as he glanced at the clouds. "Where are we going this time? I hope it's more exciting than the last place."

Indulging him for a moment, Pamina asked, "What was wrong with the last place?"

"Nothing if you don't mind hanging out in Butthole, Pennsylvania. I just so happened to mind it."

Pamina shook her head, sorry she'd asked. Why she'd gifted him with the ability to speak she'd never know.

"Because you love me," Abra said, reading her mind. "Everyone loves me."

Pamina cocked her head. "Yes, and all that loving is what landed you here with me in the first place."

"You're such a killjoy," Abra huffed.

"As God of Lust and Everything Desirous, you were supposed to help other men with women, not help yourself to them."

"Ah, but now I only have eyes for you, Pamina."

She resisted the urge to roll her own eyes.

Abra got quiet for a moment before adding, "Come on, Pamina, turn me back into a man and let me put a little bit, or rather, a *big* bit of joy into your life."

Pamina bit back a grin, no need to encourage his bad-boy behavior. Ever since Abra had crossed the boundaries while in human form, she'd been gifted—or rather cursed—with taking care of him until he could learn to control his urges. After all, as gods and goddesses they were supposed to be above reproach.

Ignoring him, she leaned out the window and perused the clouds. Her white cotton dress caught a slight breeze and ruffled around her ankles. "It looks like we're going to a small town called Mason Creek, Connecticut." She tapped Abra's nose. "Plenty of mice for you to eat, I'm sure."

Never one to enjoy her humor, Abra shivered. "Very funny. Caviar yes, mice no." He twisted around, offering her his back.

Pamina narrowed her eyes and chuckled at her ornery friend. She peered deeper into the clouds, taking in the sight of the three young, jaded women who had unknowingly beckoned her services. Not only had the women been best friends since childhood, they also all owned and operated Styles for Living, Mason Creek's bustling interior-design shop.

Pamina studied them on this beautiful morning as they window-shopped on Main Street. Dressed in black leather pants with knee high boots to match, Lindsay Bell, the tallest of the three, had an air of *bad girl* about her. She peered through the window of Toys4Gals, an adult-only toy store. Brown eyes wide, she pulled a long strand of chestnut-colored hair from her cheek and turned to face her two friends and business partners. "Like I said, just because we've sworn off men, certainly doesn't mean we have to shut down the candy shop, girls."

Tapping one perfectly manicured nail on the shop window, she pointed to an elongated, battery-operated device. "Meet Bob," she said with a smirk. "He is going to be my newest best friend."

Pamina grinned at Lindsay's antics, noting that her smart mouth and sassy attitude completed the bad-girl package. Merging their minds as one, Pamina sifted through Lindsay's thoughts, learning that she had a habit of dating men who'd done little more than scrounge off her. Men who wouldn't know a hard day's work if it jumped up and bit them on their asses and who were more than happy to dip into her meager savings.

Anna Deveau raised one brow. "Bob?" she asked. Pamina turned her attention to the petite blonde. She took a moment to study her, gauging Anna's response to Lindsay's carefree sexual attitude. Anna worried her bottom lip, pushed her hands into her jeans pockets, and glanced up and down Main Street, seemingly embarrassed by the whole conversation.

"Bob stands for 'battery-operated boyfriend'," Candace Steele piped up, perfect white teeth flashing in a smile. "I think I'll get one of those." Toying with her long dark ponytail, she went up on the balls of her gym shoes and pressed her nose to the glass. Her green eyes lit with curiosity. "I wonder if it comes with extra batteries." Then she added, "Now that I'm off men I'm going to need something to increase my heart rate and metabolism."

Lindsay snorted and rolled her eyes heavenward. "Come on, Candace. Not everything has to be about your triathlons. This toy is designed to give you an orgasm, not to help you run faster, or longer."

Candace winked at her friend. "Well, you know how I hate to peter out halfway through a race."

Pamina took a moment to sift through Candace's mind. It appeared the young athletic girl with a penchant for marathon sex attracted guys who were after her daddy's connections and influence. They claimed to love her, but time and time again, Candace discovered otherwise.

"Um, we should go," Anna squeaked out, color flooding her cheeks.

Lindsay twisted sideways and ruffled the lapels of Anna's

pristine white shirt. "You need to loosen up, girlfriend. Now that we're all off men, you're going to have to take matters into your own hands whether you like it or not." Lindsay clicked her tongue and snapped her fingers. "And as my mother always said, when you want the job done right, you have to do it yourself."

When Anna gave her friend a mortified look, Pamina surfed through her mind. Sweet romantic, Anna, a woman who, strangely enough, had a habit of attracting self-serving men. The men she had deemed boyfriends cared only about their own needs and desires, squashing her lifelong belief that she'd be swept off her feet by her very own Prince Charming and live happily ever after.

Pamina gave a resigned shake of her head and absentmindedly stroked her cat's black fur. She drew a deep breath and let it out slowly. "Honestly, it's no wonder they've sworn off men, Abra."

Considering the best approach to help these girls, she scanned Mason Creek and calculated her next move. When she came across an old, rundown Victorian house on the outskirts of town, a plan began to formulate, to take shape and pattern inside her mind.

Pamina reached outside her window and twisted a juicy red apple from the branch. Ah yes, the old house would provide the perfect setting for seduction. With that last thought in mind, she closed her eyes and bit into the apple, preparing herself for the shift. In the next instant, she reopened her lids and found herself standing on the sidewalk staring up at the old Victorian home.

It was time to pair each girl with their match and watch the sexual sparks fly.

With everything in place, she angled her head and glanced

at a very disgruntled, very bedraggled, Abra. Much aggrieved, he tossed her a miffed look. Pamina resisted the urge to chuckle. Oops, she'd forgotten to warn him of the shift.

Before Abra had time to go to work on his tattered fur, she hastily smoothed down her white cotton dress and with a lighthearted bounce to her step said, "Come on, Abra. It's not time to be worrying about your appearance. We have a lot of work to do."

Chapter One

Nose crinkled in distaste, Lindsay Bell pushed open the car door and climbed from the passenger seat. She stepped to the curb, shaded the late-afternoon sun from her eyes and perused the huge, rundown Victorian home outside of town. The place looked like a designer's worst nightmare, or a designer's dream come true, depending on whom you were asking. Lips curled in aversion, Lindsay pinched her eyes shut and feigned a shiver.

Low-slung branches fringed the perimeter of the sunburnt yard, while unkempt vines coiled around the moss-laden veranda like snakes. White paint chips trickled from the tall wooden support posts and settled like snow on the faded blue deck. Overgrown shrubs, weeds, and fallen leaves camouflaged the long, insect-infested walkway. Crickets, grasshoppers and a few other unidentified pests scurried about in their fertile playground.

When Anna stepped onto the curb beside her, Lindsay angled her head to cast her a glance. "Are you sure this is the place?" She cut her hand through the air. "It doesn't look like anyone has lived here for years."

Anna furrowed her brow and nibbled on her bottom lip. She studied the paper in her hand, then read the rusty brass numbers dangling from the cedar shingles. "This is the address she gave."

"Let me see that." Without haste, Candace circled her Honda Civic, grabbed the paper and scanned it. "91 Oak Street." She looked at the house and, with an open hand, gestured toward the front door. Never one to waste precious time, she said, "Then I guess this is it, ladies. Shall we?"

Lindsay pivoted on the ball of her foot and followed. Her very conventional, very *so-not-her* pumps tapped a steady beat as she trailed behind Candace's long, athletic strides. She shifted uncomfortably in her business attire. God, she hated having to play dress-up when interviewing new clients. She much preferred her comfortable leather pants and knee-length boots. She turned to Anna, who kept pace beside her.

"What exactly did this woman say to you when she called yesterday?"

Anna smoothed her short blonde hair behind her ears, a familiar habit of hers. "Not much, just that she was interested in restoring the old Victorian house into an inn and that she wanted to see us ASAP. When I told her we had other clients before her..." Anna stopped to rub her thumb and index finger together, "...she made us an offer we couldn't refuse."

Lindsay dropped her hand from her forehead, giving her eyes time to adjust to the late-afternoon brightness, and then carefully climbed the dilapidated stairs. She tucked her flirty blue skirt around her knees, taking care not to touch the moldy weathered railings.

"Well, no one says we have to take the offer," Lindsay said, already deciding she'd rather pass on the contract. Pulling her toenails off with pliers would be less painful than taking this place from ordinary to extraordinary. They had enough work to last them until Christmas as it was. Exorbitant amounts of money or not, Lindsay would rather decline. And she was pretty certain no one was going to change her mind on that point, obstinate witch that she was. Of course, they'd all have to consult with one another first and come to a unanimous decision.

Anna adjusted her leather briefcase over her shoulder and longingly ran her hands over the paint-chipped posts. "Are you kidding me, Lindsay? This old house is absolutely fantastic. A designer's gold mine. Just think what we could do to restore it to its natural state."

Lindsay pursed her lips and took a moment to consider things further. Hmmm...maybe Anna was on to something. After practicing celibacy for the last two months, a project of this magnitude might help keep her thoughts off men and remedy all her sexual longings. Not that her thoughts were always on men, or sex, or men and sex, mind you. Nope. Not at all.

Hell, who was she kidding? Keeping her mind off men and sex was like nailing jelly to a wall.

The truth was, no matter how much she loved the feel of skin on skin, flesh on flesh, she didn't want to have anything more to do with those lazy, good-for-nothing bastards who were more than happy to separate her from her hard-earned money. Honestly, she didn't care one iota if she ever felt the weight of a man's body on hers, or his fingers caressing her body, his mouth massaging her breasts or the soft blade of his tongue between her quivering thighs.

Lindsay swallowed a tortured moan.

Too bad she wasn't into one-night stands. Sex without relationships. Now that really was the way to go.

Anna's voice pulled her back and helped marshal her thoughts. "I can't wait to dig in," Anna said, with bright-eyed enthusiasm.

Lindsay shook her head to clear it, turned her focus back

19

to housezilla and joined Candace on the landing. Anna came up behind her, her hand trailing lovingly over the wooden porch, her eyes glazing in heavenly bliss.

Despite herself, Lindsay smiled as she watched her friend in mute fascination. Sweet, adorable Anna. She'd been a dreamer since high school, a girl who believed in fairy tales and Prince Charming. Well, a girl who *used* to believe in fairy tales and Prince Charming. Until that last self-serving jerk she'd dated had finally broken her of that delusion. Despite having completely different views on life, Lindsay loved Anna with all her heart. Which was why she'd nearly ripped that last asshole a new one after he'd hurt her. No one hurt her girls and got away with it.

When all three reached the door, Candace raised her hand to knock. Before she had a chance, the big old door swung wide open. The rusty brass hinges creaked and moaned like a wounded animal.

"Good afternoon, ladies."

"Good afternoon," they all responded in kind.

After a round of handshakes and an exchange of names, they all fell silent. Even the resident insects stopped chirping. For a long moment the woman—Pamina, as she'd introduced herself—said nothing, she just stood there taking her time to peruse each girl in turn as though assessing them. They, too, did the same.

Lindsay's gaze panned the woman before them. Tall and gorgeous, with a knee-length dress hanging loosely over her perfect slim body, Pamina had flawless skin and mystical green eyes. Her long golden hair was haphazardly piled on her head like a halo, making her look angelic. Undoubtedly, the same 'do on Lindsay would have the hair police hunting her down with a bottle of hairspray and pair of scissors. But this woman, with her heart-shaped face and creamy complexion, could likely pull off bald—and make it fashionable.

As Lindsay scrutinized Pamina, her hand went to her windblown, temperamental curls and in that instant she made up her mind.

She hated her.

Those magnificent eyes of hers, however, continued to draw Lindsay's attention. They looked as though they could read her every secret, her every dark fantasy.

Lindsay shivered, pretty damn sure that her deepest darkest fantasies would offend this sweet woman's sensibilities.

Pamina broke the silence, waved a delicate hand. "Where are my manners? Please come in. I've made lemonade and apple muffins."

Lemonade and apple muffins?

"I've been waiting for you lovely and talented ladies."

Lovely and talented?

Lindsay planted her hands on her hips. Ah hell, how could she possibly hate someone so adorable, someone so considerate, and someone so bang-on with her observations?

The oak floorboards creaked with each step as they all followed her into the kitchen. Returning to professional mode, Lindsay analyzed the interior, admiring the large rooms with their high ceilings, and the gorgeous winding staircase. Taken by the home's inner beauty, her designer's eye lit with passion, and her mind began racing with a million ideas. As Candace and Anna seated themselves, she took an extra moment to study the home, envisioning it as a bustling Victorian inn. Interest piqued, she wondered what ideas Pamina had in mind for its restoration.

"I'm sure you're all wondering what restoration ideas I have in mind."

Lindsay narrowed her gaze. Not only was the woman perfect in every way imaginable, it now appeared she could read minds too. Lindsay was leaning toward hate again until she caught the scent of freshly baked apple muffins. Yummy.

"You read my mind," Lindsay piped up, joining Candace and Anna at the long table.

Once they were all seated, Pamina pulled a fresh tray of muffins from the oven and handed them out. "Please enjoy." Without preamble she picked up her fat black cat, took a seat at the head of the table and got right to the point. "As I mentioned to Anna on the phone, I'm interested in turning this place into an inn."

Lindsay mulled the idea over again, still certain they'd decline the offer, especially with all the work piling up on their desks. They had quite a few contracted jobs that just could not wait.

Redirecting her focus, Lindsay bit into her delicious muffin and moaned, offering Pamina only half her attention.

"An inn for lovers," Pamina added, a mischievous glint in her eye.

Lovers?

Lindsay chewed, her interest picking up.

"With fantasy-inspired theme rooms."

Fantasy-inspired theme rooms?

Lindsay choked. *O-kay*, now that gained her full concentration.

Was the sweet, angelic woman talking about *sexually* inspired fantasy theme rooms? Obviously she'd been too busy making love to her muffin to understand correctly.

Before she could ask, Pamina clarified, "Yes, sexually

inspired fantasy theme rooms."

"You're kidding?" Lindsay sputtered, glancing at her coworkers. Candace leaned forward, grinning, anxiously awaiting the details. Eyes wide, Anna's mouth gaped open, color creeping up her neck.

"No, I'm not kidding." Pamina brushed a golden wisp of hair from her eyes. "What I want from you ladies is for each of you to take one of the bedrooms and using your deepest, darkest imagination, design a lover's fantasy theme room that would appeal to your sensibilities. Your budget is as unlimited as your creativity."

Lindsay's mind raced. Leather wrist cuffs, tether restraints, pleasure whips, nipple clamps. What a wickedly delicious idea for an inn.

Candace spoke up. "Our room can be anything we desire?"

Pamina nodded. "Yes."

Hell yeah!

Lindsay fought a grin. She could hardly believe this woman was going to pay her to create the perfect BDSM room, something she'd always longed to do for herself, but never had the space in her small condo, or the funds needed to purchase the equipment. Not to mention the right man to share it with.

Lindsay arched one brow. This was like her designer dream job come true. "Are you serious?" Surely to God the woman was messing with her mind.

Pamina nodded again. "One hundred percent."

Hot damn! She was serious. One hundred percent.

That settled it. She loved this woman.

Pamina waited a moment, as though letting them digest the information. "So what do you say, ladies, are you interested in the contract?"

Okay, so maybe the other jobs *could* wait.

Heck, if she wasn't getting any hot monkey loving, at least she could live vicariously through her imagination and let other couples enjoy the fruits of her labor.

"Well...?" Pamina asked.

Without consulting with her partners, Lindsay blurted, "We'll take it."

Chapter Two

Hands in her pockets, Lindsay walked the perimeter of the upstairs bedroom and wondered why Pamina had chosen such a small room for her to decorate. How she was going to fit an eclectic mix of bondage equipment in such a tight space, she'd never know. She angled her head, envisioning the design and layout. Damn, it just wasn't going to work. The king-sized headboard alone would eat up half the space. Not to mention the padded bench and love swing that she'd ordered earlier that morning. Lord, if two people engaged in a little lighthearted sexual play in such cramped quarters, someone was liable to put an eye out.

Just then Pamina's fat black cat, Abra, sauntered into the room. Purring, he jumped onto the windowsill and with his piercing feline eyes, watched her every movement. His low purr grew louder and louder, as though demanding her undivided attention.

Lindsay stepped up to him. "Okay, okay." Good Lord, how the heck was she supposed to concentrate while he made such a racket? After a couple of quick strokes of his silky fur, she crossed her arms and turned her attention back to the drab walls, considering her options. Pushing away from the window, she trailed her hand along one papered wall until she came across a tattered seam. Using a long manicured nail, she worked the edge free and ripped, disheartened to find six or more layers underneath. It'd be a bitch to peel, but at least only one of the four walls had paper on it. The other three were painted in a brownish yellow color that reminded her of doggy droppings. Ugh. It had to go. Lindsay envisioned deep, dark earthy tones as a backdrop to soft sconce lighting and mirrored walls and ceilings.

Pondering the task before her, she joined Abra on the windowsill. Although she'd never had an affinity for cats, and this one actually kind of creeped her out with his inquisitive eyes, she scooped him into her arms and sized him up.

Feigning exhaustion after lifting him, she drew a ragged breath. "Good Lord, Abra, I think we're going to have to talk to Candace about getting you on a regular exercise program. Maybe you could go with her on one of her runs." Lindsay reached under his belly and grabbed a fistful of fat cat. "Either that or you're going to have to get out and find yourself a girlfriend and work off some of this extra padding."

Ignoring her, he nestled his chubby little body into her arms, where he lazily proceeded to groom himself. Lindsay shook her head as he thoroughly disregarded her.

Typical male.

Shifting her thoughts to the task at hand, Lindsay inspected the room once again. Her gaze settled on the only piece of furniture, an ugly, yellow oversized recliner, which practically took up the whole space. That had to go too.

"What do you think, Abra?" She cut her hand through the air. "Too small?" Abra purred and nestled his face against her chest. His whiskers tickled her skin as his rough tongue lapped at her cleavage like it was a saucer of milk. Startled, she leapt from the windowsill and gasped.

"Whoa there, big guy." She eased his head away, feeling a

little perverted at the way her nipples tightened. Okay, obviously it had been far too long since a man had given her breasts a tongue bath.

When she met Abra's blue almond-shaped eyes, his tongue darted out to lick his lips, and she could have sworn he just winked at her. "You really are a typical male, aren't you? One-track mind, straight for the milk jugs."

"Will you never learn?"

Pamina's voice sounded at the doorway. As if he'd been caught with his hand in the cookie jar, or rather his face buried in Lindsay's breasts, Abra jumped to the floor and scurried into the hall.

Pamina arched a brow, her lips thinned to a fine line. "Not so fast, pal." She scooped him up before he could dart down the staircase and cast him a look that suggested he was in all kinds of trouble. For a moment Lindsay pondered their strange relationship.

Suddenly someone stepped up behind Pamina and gained Lindsay's full attention. A very big, very brawny, very slurpalicious someone. And no longer was Pamina and Abra's strange relationship of any interest to her.

Pamina moved farther into the room, the mysterious stranger shadowing her movements. Captivated by Pamina's new friend, Lindsay scraped her teeth over her bottom lip and watched his strong, athletic body move with self-confidence and assuredness. When he circled Pamina and came around to face Lindsay, their gazes connected and locked. In that moment something sparked between them and a weird tingling began in her bloodstream.

Lindsay didn't believe in love at first sight, nor did she believe in fate or destiny, but this guy, wow, this guy with his mesmerizing blue eyes could suck her under like a tsunami wave and make her believe in anything.

He smiled and Lindsay's pulse leapt in her throat. Her lascivious, sex-deprived body immediately shifted into overdrive. One seductive look from him had her hormones firing at jet speed in record time.

His long athletic gait closed the space between them. As he stood before her, she tipped her head and pulled his spicy, panty-soaking aroma into her lungs, letting it wrap around her, letting it arouse all her senses. Lord, the man just oozed sexuality and testosterone.

Her gazed panned the length of him, stopping to inspect his broad shoulders, trim waist and rock-hard thighs. She wondered for a second if anything else under those snug jeans was rock hard. Damned if she didn't want to find out.

Whew!

Had the temperature in the room suddenly skyrocketed?

Once again her hungry gaze traveled back to his face, taking in his dark features, unkempt shoulder-length hair, with bangs that swished to the side, square jaw and unshaven face. The guy had bad boy written all over him. Lindsay knew his type well. A Casanova who was, undoubtedly, so very, very good. Just the kind of guy she knew better than to get involved with.

Despite that, lust rose to the surface, clamoring for attention and all she could think of was men. Sex. Men and sex. And not necessarily in that order. Forget nailing jelly to the wall. She wanted this guy to nail *her* to the wall.

Right here.

Right now.

Of course, this is what she got for going without sex for the last two months. It appeared that a quick trip back to

Toys4Gals to pick up extra batteries and maybe even a few new gadgets was definitely in order. She made a mental note to put that at the top of her to-do list.

Mr. Slurpalicious gave her a sexy, predatory smile that screamed of the big bad wolf—and of even bigger and badder things they could do together. Libidinous slut that she was, she pondered for a moment if he would gobble her up like a frosted cupcake. Or if he'd lay her out like a buffet and take his time to savor her like a rich, decadent dessert.

Yummy.

After a thorough inspection of his tall, brawny body, her gaze went to his big hands. Damn, there was just something about a man's hands that got her juices flowing like a broken dam. She noted that he had a working man's hands, different from the soft, pampered hands of the good-for-nothing bastards she had a habit of attracting. Lindsay afforded herself a minute to visualize how those rough, callused palms of his would feel on her naked flesh, on her breasts, between her thighs. Oh yeah! She shivered. Almost violently.

A man like him could make her abandon her vow to stay away from men. She furrowed her brow and sifted through her memories. Why again was it that she'd made that vow?

When Pamina touched his muscular arm and he turned, giving her his undivided attention, a weird pang of jealousy cut through Lindsay.

"I'd like you to meet Lindsay Bell," Pamina said. "She's the brilliant interior designer I hired to turn this space into a BDSM room for lovers."

Lips curved up at the corners, he angled his head, clearly intrigued. "Oh yeah?"

Heat arced between them as he stepped closer and held his arm out. Her body responded to his proximity. Pleasure raced through her and she became hyper-aware of dampness between her thighs. Had she been wearing panties, they'd have been soaked.

She attempted to rein in her desire, to pull herself together and abandon her lusty thoughts, she really did. But so far her efforts were proving futile.

His sensual mouth slanted and the gleam in his eyes held all sorts of promises. "A BDSM room. How interesting. I look forward to seeing the end results."

She made one more attempt to gather control over her wayward thoughts, but his deep sensuous voice shattered all her efforts. In fact his rich tone sent her tortured, hormonal body into convulsions. Her nipples tightened painfully, heat and hunger lapped at her thighs.

It suddenly occurred to her he was waiting for a handshake. With little finesse, she thrust her arm forward and slipped her hand inside his. His huge palm practically swallowed hers up. As her flesh absorbed his heat, her libido roared to life in a way it never had before. Christ, she knew she had a healthy sexual appetite, but the sudden cravings for this man both frightened and excited her.

She schooled her features into polite interest while her hormones danced to the beat of that eighties AC/DC song "You Shook Me All Night Long".

"I'm Lindsay," she said.

He grinned and shot her a wolfish look. Assuring her, that with a huff and a puff he could blow her house down. Except it wasn't a house Lindsay was interested in him blowing. Damn, this celibacy thing was definitely playing havoc with her body...and her mind. She needed to get her thoughts off sex and on to the conversation at hand.

"I'm Lindsay," she repeated.

"I know," he said. "Lindsay Bell."

"How do you know my name?" Looking for a distraction, anything to get her mind off Mr. Sexy Pants, Lindsay grabbed the overstuffed chair and began to slide it toward the doorway. Damn, the thing was heavy.

"Pamina already introduced you." His slow smile licked over her thighs and filled her mind with wild and wicked images.

Right! Damn. She was making a total ass of herself, which was something she never did. Christ, no man had ever had that effect on her before. She'd always maintained a cool, in-charge demeanor.

She strived for normalcy and tried not to stumble over her words. "And you are?" she asked, expecting his name to begin with big and end in wolf. *Expecting?* Okay, okay, maybe *hoping* was a better choice of words.

"I'm Brad Caldwell."

Damn.

His gaze roamed over her and his deep, big-bad-wolf tone sent shivers skittering down her spine, making her suddenly wish she was draped in a red cape and covered in icing.

"Pamina asked me to stop by to chat with you."

"Oh?" Lindsay turned to face Pamina, heavy chair forgotten.

Pamina waved one delicate hand through the air. "I thought Brad could take down that wall and open this room up for you."

Lindsay glanced at the papered wall and considered that option. Not a bad idea. "That would certainly beat the hell out of peeling all that paper off."

Face locked in concentration, Brad stepped up to the wall and ran his fingers over the aged paper. Lindsay's stomach tightened and her knees weakened as she envisioned him running his hands over her body just like that.

Oh my!

Common sense dictated that she decline the offer and make do with the small room. Yeah, that's exactly what she'd do. Decline Pamina's suggestion to take down the wall and just make the best out of the cramped quarters. Because having him around for the next week or so would simply distract her and play havoc with her hormones. And since she'd sworn off men, it was a distraction she didn't want or need. No way. No how.

Brad turned to face her. "So, what do you say, Lindsay? Would you like me to hang around and take down that wall for you?"

Hang around.

Take down the wall.

Strip her naked.

Have his wicked way with her.

With casual nonchalance, he rolled one broad shoulder. "I could even help you out with the bondage equipment, if you'd like."

Help her out? As in try it out with her?

Hell yeah, she liked.

Brad picked up the overstuffed chair and with little effort moved it into the hallway. "You know, in case you need a strong arm to lift things." His words said one thing but the heat in his eyes told an entirely different story. One that could easily get her into trouble with another bad boy. She quickly reminded herself why she'd sworn off sweet-talking playboys in the first place.

"So what do you say?" he asked again as her mind reeled.

Say no, say no.

"Yes."

Damn!

Brad blew out a breath he hadn't even realized he was holding. Sure he was relieved Lindsay had hired him. The extra funds would come in handy to help pay for his medical-school prep classes. But, he had to admit, there was one other big reason he was pleased he'd gotten the job.

And that reason was Lindsay Bell.

There was something about her. The minute their eyes met and locked, heat simmered between them. It was a heat unlike anything he'd experienced before. A heat that he was definitely interested in exploring further. He suspected she felt it too. In fact, the way her eyes devoured him with hunger, he was most certain of it.

Lindsay Bell, smart and beautiful, with her curvaceous body, sassy outfit, and desire to create a lovers BDSM room, had bad girl written all over her.

He knew her type all too well. She was the kind of girl who'd undoubtedly see him as someone she'd be interested in delving into a brief, no-strings affair with. He'd come to expect that from women.

He knew people were quick to judge him and dub him a go-nowhere kind of guy just because he worked as a handyman in the family business—a steady, respectable business that had been handed down in the Caldwell family from generation to generation. People really had no idea what went into running such a successful operation.

Even though Brad enjoyed the labor-intensive work, he'd always had a yearning to break away from the pack and do something different with his life. Unfortunately no one in his family, or in his community, had supported his dream to become a doctor. They all thought it was ridiculous really, and even the night classes and correspondence courses he'd taken over the years to get his science degree didn't seem to sway their minds. The women he knew assumed because he swung a hammer, he was all brawn and no brains. They saw him as a great guy to have sex with, and nothing more.

Naturally everyone expected him to follow in his father's footsteps and take over his handyman business. After his father had passed away during Brad's high school years, and his mother had taken sick, Brad had done just that, needing the funds to support his two younger siblings and help take care of household finances. Sure he had to postpone medical school, but that didn't mean he'd given up his dream, not at all. It just meant he had to work extra hours outside his regular job to get enough funds to pay for his prep course.

Which had led him to Mason Creek.

To Lindsay.

He took a moment to study her. Rays of sunlight streamed through the windowpane and fell over her lush body. Her chestnut hair looked wild and uncontrolled, a little like her, he suspected. Dressed in tight-fitting jeans and a low-cut silky top, his body registered every delicious detail of the woman before him. Her natural feminine scent saturated the small bedroom. Brad inhaled, pulling it into his lungs and letting it arouse all his senses.

When Pamina touched Lindsay's arm, Lindsay turned to her. Brad's body hummed and his blood pressure soared as he glimpsed Lindsay's gorgeous, curvy backside.

Damned if she wasn't the most perfect woman he'd set eyes on.

But even if Brad wanted more with Lindsay, he saw the way she looked at him, the same way every other woman had looked at him. He knew if they hooked up, she'd only be in it for the ride. Not that he had anything against the ride, mind you. He didn't. Hell, he loved the ride. He was a healthy, red-blooded American male after all. But the truth was, he wanted more from a woman. After years of searching for that special someone, he'd given up hope in finding his perfect match. One who'd accepted him for who he really was, a small-town boy with brawn *and* brains. A woman who wanted him for more than just a quick roll in the sack and one who supported his dream to become a doctor.

He leaned back against the doorjamb and watched Lindsay discuss her decorating ideas with Pamina. Her face lit with excitement, and her dark eyes were animated as she described the layout and furniture placement. Her energy and creative insight impressed him. In fact, he might have just met her, but there were already a lot of things about Lindsay that impressed him.

And for some unfathomable reason, he suspected if he went for a quick heated ride with her, she'd turn his life upside down without even trying.

Chapter Three

For days now, Lindsay had watched Brad while he tore down the wall, enjoying the sight of a hard man, hard at work. It didn't take her long to figure out that in a lot of ways he wasn't like the men she'd dated. Not only was he dedicated and driven, he worked from sunup until sundown and wasn't afraid to get his hands dirty. He also took great care and pride in his work.

Damn, she found that sexy.

Sitting on the floor across from him, notepad in hand, she'd finished drawing out her designs and now waited patiently for her bondage equipment to arrive. No need to rush things, she mused. Not when she was perfectly happy entertaining herself by watching Brad work.

She wouldn't be able to paint or hang her mirrors until after Brad had completed his job, not with all the dust in the air. All her furniture had been ordered and her sexy BDSM props sat in a box nearby, waiting to be displayed. Lindsay planned on securing them behind glass doors in the melamine cubbyholes she'd purchased. The items were for viewing only, and should the lovers wish to purchase any of the goodies, they'd have to see Pamina, who now had her very own stockroom full. Thanks to Lindsay's favorite store, Toys4Gals.

So with nothing much to do in the interim, she wasted her

morning away by watching one shirtless, one very tanned and very muscular man tear down a wall.

Did life get any better than this?

Hell yeah! She could be half-naked too. Or better yet, completely naked.

Lust shot through her and warmed her blood as she pictured such a delightfully delicious thing. Brad's hard body on top of hers—damn how she loved the weight of a man's body pressing down on hers. His mouth claiming her, showering her hot, naked flesh with heated kisses. His silky tongue sliding downward, following a heated path to her stomach and lower, until he reached the moist apex between her legs. His wet tongue opening her swollen pink folds with the utmost expertise, so he could dip inside and taste her creamy essence. His thick fingers pushing deep inside her pussy, moving in and out, in and out, until she went up in flames beneath his perfect ministrations. Her body began thrumming with heat and desire. She swallowed a tortured moan.

Lindsay brushed a bead of perspiration from her forehead and squeezed her thighs together as a shiver of need made her quake.

She really should have sex with him. That might help ease the tremendous amount of sexual tension between them and get her focus back on her job.

Christ, she knew when she agreed to hiring such a luscious bad boy it would drive her to distraction. And such a distraction had her wavering in her vow to steer clear of men.

It didn't take long for her convictions to soften around the edges. As she pondered the situation, her lascivious gaze swept over him again. She spent a moment reasoning with herself. Sure she'd sworn off men, but that didn't mean she had to swear off sex too, right? Although one-night stands weren't her thing, couldn't she have hot, wild monkey sex with him just this once? Why complicate things with a relationship that was doomed to fail, judging by her track record, that is.

Surely she could keep her emotions under wraps while she explored his mouth, his chest, his abdomen, and any other parts of that lethally honed body that her tongue had happened to stumble upon. She licked her suddenly dry lips and suppressed a heated whimper. And really, shouldn't she try out the bondage equipment at least once before opening the lover's room to guests. Lindsay rolled her eyes heavenward.

Good Lord, talk about logical reasoning at its worst.

Needing to keep her mind off sex before she jumped up, threw herself at him and begged him for some hot loving, she abandoned her thoughts and decided to engage him in conversation. They'd been making idle chitchat for days now but being the nosey...er...inquisitive woman that she was, she wanted to know more about the real Brad Caldwell. Who was he and what made him tick?

She worked to keep her tone light. No need to let him know she'd been sitting there drooling over him all morning. Then again, the saliva pooling at the corners of her mouth was likely a dead giveaway.

Lindsay wiped her mouth. "Need any help?"

"Nope, I'm getting there," he said. "And then you can start your painting."

She crinkled her nose, admiring the job. "It's looking good so far." When he tossed her a smile she asked, "So tell me, Brad. How did you become a handyman?"

He dropped a piece of plaster onto the growing pile and angled his body to face her. "Family business. My father taught me everything I know. I had a hammer in my hand even before I could walk."

Hmmm, that must be how he got all those scrumptious muscles.

He gave a soft chuckle. "Apparently *bang bang* were my first words," he added, mimicking the actions of a hammer hitting a nail. "Or so my mother says."

She grinned, loving his playful tone and easy demeanor. As she pictured Brad as a toddler, lugging a hammer around everywhere he went, it occurred to her how easy he was to be with these last few days and how easy he was to talk to.

Lindsay leaned back against the wall and glanced at his work. "The men I attract wouldn't know a hard day's work if it jumped up and bit them on their asses."

Brad laughed out loud, which, for some strange reason, pleased her immensely.

Lindsay tossed her notepad aside, pulled her knees to her chest and hugged her legs. "I think it's great that you're a handyman."

He shot her a skeptical glance. "Really?"

"Yeah, there is nothing wrong with hard labor. My father is a plumber. When I was a kid, I went with him on a few calls. Now that's a labor-intensive job too." She got quiet for a moment as she thought about her father. She really needed to spend more time with him. "I think you two would really hit it off." She lowered her voice to mimic her father's deep, raspy tone. "As he would always say, 'a hard day's work never killed anyone and there is nothing wrong with a respectable blue-collar job'." The sudden image of introducing Brad to her parents rushed through her mind. Whoa...where the heck had that thought come from?

With the back of his hand, Brad brushed dust from his forehead. "Most women I attract don't see my job that way."

She slanted her head and stretched out her legs. "Well I'm

not most women."

He nodded, arched one brow and stared at her for a long moment. "I guess not."

Something about the way he was looking at her had her thinking of naked bodies, exploring hands and sexy bedroom noises. Lust settled deep between her legs and it was all she could do not to quiver.

He turned the questions on to her and she was thankful for the reprieve. "How did you get into interior decoration?"

Just then Abra came sauntering back into the room and eased himself onto her lap. Without conscious thought, she stroked his soft fur. "I always loved to decorate or, as my parents put it, destroy my bedroom and then put it back together at least once a week. Candace and Anna were my accomplices. When we finished my room, we'd do theirs. So it was only natural that the three of us would go into business together."

When Brad grinned, her insides turned to mush.

With a nod of his head, he gestured toward her lap. "It looks like you made a new friend."

Rolling her shoulders, she continued to stroke Abra's fur. "And to think I don't even like cats, let alone want one cuddling up with me. Obviously Abra doesn't care about what I want." She shook her head and under her breath said, "Typical male."

Brad gave her an odd look. "You can always put him out of the room."

"Nah, he's not really bothering me. He's just looking for a little loving."

Something in Brad's eyes softened. He cocked his head and gave her a warm smile. He dropped his tools and sat down next to her on the floor, the proximity creating an instant intimacy.

For the second time Lindsay felt all gooey inside, like a warm chocolate-chip cookie straight out of the oven.

"Well he sure seems to like you," Brad said, his voice whispery soft. Abra, being the ornery cat that he was, turned away from him, and snuggled tighter into Lindsay's lap.

"Lucky me. It must be my charm," she said easily, waving her hand through the air.

Brad pitched his voice low, his eyes darkened. The air around them charged with sexual energy. "I guess you have that effect on all males, Lindsay. Feline or human." His gaze brushed over her face, his blatant flirting and bold, uncensored words letting her know that he too felt a strong pull toward her.

Oh boy!

A burst of sexual awareness arced between them and set her loins on fire. She fought the urge to squirm—right onto his lap. The provocative mental image of straddling him sent heat spiraling onward and upward through her body. Liquid desire pooled between her thighs. She pulled in a fortifying breath and tried to remind herself why sex with him would be a bad thing. Dear God, this guy sure had a way of messing with her mind, and her resolve.

As though attempting to lighten the mood, Brad brought the conversation back around to Candace and Anna. "Tell me more about your friends. It sounds like the three of you are pretty close."

She drew a breath, centering herself. "Yeah, like we always said since grade school, BFFAA."

"BFFAA?"

"Best friends forever and always."

He shook his head and chuckled. "Ah, of course. How could I not have known that?"

She shot him a smart-assed look and turned the conversation back to him. "If you're from Hillside, why did you come all the way to Mason Creek for such a small job?"

Face serious, Brad spent a long moment looking at her, as though assessing her, his blue eyes intense, his jaw clenched. Then, as quickly as it had disappeared, his easy demeanor returned. With a lighthearted tone, he said, "No job is too small."

Something told her that wasn't entirely the truth. Was there more going on with Brad than he let on? Never one for subtleties, she was about to probe, but stopped herself when Anna and Candace poked their heads in.

Lindsay jumped to her feet. "Hey, girls, come on in." Lord, over the last few days, they'd all been so busy designing their own rooms they barely saw one another.

"Hey, Lindsay. Hey, Brad."

Lindsay crossed the room and gave her friends a big hug. "How are you girls making out?" She narrowed her eyes and pressed her hand to Candace's forehead. "Are you feeling okay? You look a bit flushed."

Candace shook her head. "Just hungry. Been working out...I mean, working hard."

Lindsay turned her attention to Anna and noticed that she had that old familiar dreamy look in her eyes. Good Lord, had she been dreaming of fairy tales, Prince Charming and happily-ever-after again? For a moment she wondered what they were up to in their rooms.

"Anna, are you okay?"

Anna blinked and said quickly, "We're heading out to lunch and to run a few errands. Can you join us?"

The way she'd redirected the conversation hadn't gone

unnoticed. Lindsay was about to press but the sound of a truck pulling into the driveway gained her attention. She rushed to the window to peer out. "It looks like I'll have to take a rain check, ladies. That's my equipment."

After she waved Candace and Anna away, warning them not to work too hard if they weren't feeling well, Brad piped up. "Let me help you."

Lindsay looked over her shoulder and cast him a sideways glance. "What's that?" When she caught his dark intense gaze, her entire body went up in flames. He had that look in his eyes again. One that spoke of hunger and longing, and did weird and wonderful things to her insides.

He stood, brushed the dust from his jeans and stalked toward her, closing the distance between them. As he invaded her personal space, his heated glance slid over her body like a lover's caress.

For a moment silence stretched between them, then he repeated, "Let me help you." His voice was like a low velvet seduction. When Lindsay heard the dark desire creeping into his tone, she swallowed.

Hard.

Heartbeat accelerated, she opened her eyes wide and regarded him. Her voice wobbled. "Okay" was all she managed to squeak out.

He adjusted his body so it pressed against hers. A warm palm cupped her face. His smile was slow. Inviting.

Wolfish.

Sexual tension hung heavy in the air and curled around them. "Since you love to watch me while I'm hard at work, why don't you let me carry in your equipment and really give you a show." She saw the mischief in his eyes.

Oh. Good. God.

He looked like he was going to eat her alive.

And heaven help her, she'd like nothing better.

Chapter Four

Two hours later, after they had carried in all the furniture and put together a gigantic king-sized bed, Brad stood back and watched Lindsay straddle her brand-new padded bench. Long legs spread wide on either side of the elongated black piece of bondage equipment, a smile lighting up her gorgeous brown eyes. Bouncy chestnut curls fell over her shoulders and tumbled in silken waves as she twisted her head back and forth admiring all the new toys.

Desire slammed through him as he took in the erotic vision before him. Of course, there was only one problem with the picture. Lindsay still had her clothes on, and her arms and legs weren't bound.

His cock grew hard thinking about it.

Brad studied Lindsay a moment longer. There was no denying they both wanted each other. The sexual tension between them was palpable. The room had been buzzing with sexually charged electricity since the minute they'd met.

He crossed his arms and leaned against the doorjamb, pondering her desire to create a lovers' BDSM room.

The more he thought of it, the more he realized Lindsay really didn't seem the type to design such a fantasy-inspired theme room. Although he was only just getting to know her, he suspected she wasn't the sort who'd want to be the dominant.

Which left him with only one conclusion. She herself wanted to be dominated. He'd spent enough time with her to see the image she put to the world. Strong, bold, take-charge kind of girl, one who wouldn't like to have her control stripped away.

The way one would while playing bondage games.

How interesting.

He paused to speculate a moment longer. Although Lindsay at first appeared to be like every other woman he'd met, a woman who was only interested in fucking him, he was beginning to have his doubts. Maybe, just maybe there was more to her than met the eye. Over the past few days he started to suspect it, but his suspicions were confirmed earlier when she began to talk about her father and her admiration and respect for his job.

The truth was, the two had totally hit it off and he liked everything about her, especially the way she cared for and supported her family and friends. Those qualities meant a great deal to him.

He considered his sudden epiphany longer. Yeah, he was pretty damn certain she had more going on inside than she let on.

Lindsay ran her hands along the bench. Her words pulled him from his musings. "This is perfect, just what I was hoping for."

His cock throbbed as he gazed at her curvy body. There was absolutely no doubt he wanted her between the sheets, but he also wondered if there could be more between them than just physical act of sex. Damned if he didn't want to find out.

And he knew of one way for him to do that. By helping her test out her bondage equipment. Because he suspected then and only then would he be able to strip away her layers and get her to open up to him, physically and emotionally, and in the process find out if they'd connect on a deeper level.

Lindsay swung her long leg to one side, stood, and began to slide the heavy bench under the window. "You think you can give me a hand with this?"

Getting right to the heart of the matter, he ignored her question and asked one of his own. "Why a BDSM room, Lindsay?"

"I thought it would be fun." She hedged the real truth, he guessed.

"You're a strong, take-charge kind of girl, but something tells me you're not interested in dominating a guy."

Task momentarily forgotten, she stood, rolled one shoulder, her voice casual. "I'm not."

So his suspicions *were* right.

"You also don't *act* like the kind of girl who'd want to give up control so easily."

She angled her chin in defiance, her voice full of conviction. "I don't."

Brad shrugged, pushed off the doorframe and gripped the doorknob. "Exactly, so then why BDSM?" He presumed that giving up control was exactly what she wanted. He'd seen her with her friends, although only briefly, but enough to know that Lindsay always took care of everyone else, but maybe deep down she wanted to let go of that control and have someone else take the reins for a change.

Fortunately for him, this gave him the perfect opportunity to give her what she'd always wanted, and in the process break down her defenses and find out if they were destined to be together.

Flustered, she folded her arms. "Are you going to go all Dr. Phil on me or are you going to help me move this bench?"

He shut the door. Lindsay's eyes widened at the sound of the lock clicking in place. He could almost see her body stir to life. Almost hear her mind reeling with possibilities.

"What—"

In two long strides he closed the distance between them and pressed his fingers to her lips. "Shh."

He watched her throat work as she swallowed and knew, by the heated look in her eyes, her untamed passion and desires matched his. She wanted this as much as he did. No questions about it.

He gripped her slim waist and packaged her soft body against his. Christ, she felt so incredible in his arms, he could only imagine how wonderful she'd feel trapped between his legs. Nudging her feet with his, he backed her up until the rear of her knees hit the padded table. Eyes wide, questioning, her chest rose and fell with her erratic breathing.

He tugged her T-shirt out from her tight jeans. When his fingers connected with her soft skin, his brain nearly shut down. "I'm going to give you what you want, Lindsay."

Her voice hitched, color bloomed high on her cheeks. "How do you know what I want?" He heard the intrigue in her voice and felt her hips push against him. It was a slight movement but hadn't gone unnoticed.

He offered her a slow smile. "You're going to have to trust me on that one."

"I can't possibly see—"

He pitched his voice low and demanded in a deep tone. "Take off your clothes. Nice and slow." He touched her arm and felt her body shake with excitement.

"You've got to be kidding me?" Her voice betrayed her emotions. He could see the passion, the invitation building in her eyes.

He shook his head. "Not even for a minute."

"Brad—"

"Take them off, Lindsay. Now. Nice and slow like I told you. If you don't follow the rules, I'm afraid you'll be punished."

He slid his hand between her legs and cupped her sex, just to prove just how serious he was.

An edgy laugh morphed into a heated moan. He noted the way her legs wobbled. "*Sweet mother of God,*" she whispered under her breath. Then she starched her spine and met his glace. "What if I don't want to?" Her voice lacked conviction. They both knew it.

He trailed his finger over her arm and felt the goose bumps on her flesh. "You do. Now take them off. Then I want you sprawled out on that bench. I want you naked, hot and wet, and begging me to fuck you."

"Ohmigod," he heard her gasp as his lips closed over hers for a deep, intense, mind-numbing kiss. He slipped his tongue inside her delicious mouth and spent a long moment just tasting her lush sweetness. Jesus, he wanted to devour her. All of her. Right now.

Lindsay inched back, her eyes clouded with emotion, her voice breathless. "This can only be about sex, Brad. Just to help ease the tension between us. Nothing more."

"Naturally," he agreed, lightheartedly, feeling anything but. He might have readily agreed with her, but the truth was, he wanted to see where this led them. With that he gave her a gentle push.

Lindsay landed on the bench, her legs spread. Brad let out an agonized groan as his groin tightened and throbbed in heated anticipation. Jesus, he'd never felt such intense desire before. It took all his strength and willpower not to act on his natural urges and answer the demands of his body. At the moment he'd like nothing more than to strip her clothes off, spread her legs wide open and sink his cock into her damp heat. Honestly, it practically killed him not to ravish her caveman style, to push inside her pussy and fuck her until sundown. But, right now, this was about Lindsay, so he needed to control those urges for the time being.

He growled low in his throat as she sat there, eyes glazed with lust as she awaited his instructions. God dammit he wanted her. So much so that he ached to the point of pain. He took a moment to get himself under control before he fucked her with wild abandon.

Obviously not wanting to give him time to catch up and anxious to get the game started, she asked, "What is it you'd like me to do?"

It didn't take her long to assume her role of submissive, which led him to believe she'd been fantasizing about this for quite some time. It also led him to believe no man had ever taken the time to get to know her on a deeper lever and understand her needs and desires. Stupid bastards. With a girl this incredible, this amazing, a guy had to be a total asshole not to spend all his time getting to know the real her. And give her what she wanted.

"Take you pants off and then resume that position."

Lindsay obliged without hesitation. She lowered herself onto her back and brought her legs onto the bench. She unsnapped her pants, pulled the zipper and wiggled her gorgeous, curvy ass. Once her jeans were at her ankles she kicked them away. Without inhibition, she sprawled across the bench. He was pleased at how comfortable she was in her own skin. He met her glance. The look in her eyes conveyed without words just how excited she was. Which pleased him immensely.

Brad walked around her, devouring her with his eyes. With exquisite gentleness, he touched her bare legs, his fingers trailing lightly over her soft skin, going higher and higher, coming perilously close to her pussy. Her body quaked. Her legs inched open in invitation.

He lowered his voice. "Very, very nice." He inhaled and could already smell the tang of her arousal.

"Brad please," she begged, and reached for him, her fingers brushing against his throbbing cock.

He shackled her hands and put them to her sides. "Sit up," he commanded. "And take off your shirt."

Lindsay sat up, her legs wide open, straddling the bench. As he took in the sight of her, he thought he'd go mad with want. The need to fuck her made him edgy, shaky.

He swallowed and worked to control his voice. "Spread your legs wider." She did, but it wasn't nearly wide enough for him to have a full, unobstructed view of her sweet spot. "Wider, Lindsay," he whispered his glance going to the unpacked box of BDSM toys in the corner of the room. "If you're not going to listen, I'll have to punish you."

Her face flushed from heat, her dark eyes glazed with passion. A soft mewl caught in her throat. He stroked her again. Her body buzzed, her skin felt hot to the touch.

She shimmied to the end of the bench and spread her legs impossibly wider, offering her pussy up to him so nicely.

"That's a girl."

Twin folds opened for him, affording him a view of her luscious pink softness. Jesus, her pussy was drenched with desire. He did this to her. Damn that pleased him, knowing he could raise her passions to such height and make her soaked with need.

He lowered himself to his knees to get a better look. He leaned in and inhaled, pulling her feminine scent into his lungs. Then he blew a warm breath over her pussy. Her damp hairs bristled.

She drew a shaky breath. "Oh God," she whispered and tilted her pelvis forward, an obvious plea for more.

Her heat beckoned him and he wanted to touch her. No. He needed to touch her. If he didn't soon feel her softness, he was certain an artery would blow. His jeans tightened painfully reminding him just how much he wanted her, just how much she affected him. Brad couldn't ever remember feeling so crazed, so out of control.

He drew a breath, gathering himself. "You are incredible, babe," he breathed the words over her pussy and watched her sex muscles tighten and throb.

After a light brush of his knuckle over her swollen clit, his finger moved to her moist opening. He probed her pussy and knew, as well as he knew his own name, that once he entered her, once she branded him with her heat, he'd never be the same again. With her hips bucking forward, she drove his finger inside.

"Jesus," he said, loving the way the tight walls of her pussy closed over him. He'd never felt anything so divine.

Brad pressed a finger inside her, unmoving. His gaze went to her shirt. "Didn't I tell you to take your top off?"

"Yes, but—"

"Shh," he silenced with a frown. "Don't question me. Just do as I say." His glance went to the box of toys a second time. "Otherwise, you'll be punished."

He could feel light ripples inside her pussy, a telltale sign that punishment was exactly what she wanted. With hurried hands, she gripped her shirt and pulled it off, exposing a pretty red satin bra.

Shaky fingers went to her bra straps, but he stopped her. After all, she wasn't the only one with fantasies. "Leave it on." He wiggled his finger inside her slightly, rewarding her for her obedience.

Her hands fell to her lap, her head lolled to the side. A deep moan rose up from the depths of her throat. "That feels so good, Brad."

A second finger joined the first. He pushed deep inside her until he found her G-spot. With a light brush, he stroked her until her body quivered. He knew she was close, so close to release. But since it was too soon for her to tumble over, he pulled his fingers out.

Her lids flew open. "Brad, no," she cried but her voice fell off when she caught the way he was looking at her nipples, which were so hard they almost poked through the thin material of her bra.

Brad climbed out from between her legs and circled her. "Stand up."

She did as he requested. His gaze took in the gorgeous sight of the naked woman before him. "You are so beautiful."

He watched her glance pan over him. "Please, Brad. Take your clothes off. Let me look at you."

He narrowed his eyes. "I don't remember giving you permission to speak."

One measured step brought him face to face with her. He gripped her bra and tugged the cups down, until they settled below her full breasts. Her eyes brimmed with desire when he licked his lips.

Gorgeous, prominent nipples jutted out at him, demanding attention. He bent forward and ran his tongue over them, taking his sweet time to savor her exquisite taste and texture. Damn she tasted like a vine-ripened peach, his favorite. He straightened and then plucked one hard bud with his fingertips, until it swelled and darkened.

A shaky hand reached out and closed over his thick cock and squeezed. Her fingers reached underneath to massage his balls through his jeans.

Fuck. Her touch nearly drove him to his knees.

With effort, he inched back and scolded. "I didn't give you permission to touch me."

She groaned and spread her legs, as though welcoming whatever punishment he deemed fit.

Brad circled his arms around her and walked her backwards, until her sweet ass touched the windowsill. "Stay there."

He backed up and turned his attention to the box in the corner. He tore open the top and peered inside. "Well, well, what do we have here?" As he perused the toys, he heard her breath catch. Brad pulled out a set of clamps that he could only surmise went on her nipples, and something that looked like a flogger. Hell, he'd seen enough adult movies to know what to do with that.

He turned back to her, their gazes locked, her eyes holding so much pleasure, so much emotion. Seeing that look on her face and knowing he'd put it there stirred the primal male inside him. His primitive urges roared to life.

"Turn around and press your hands to the window." When she did as he asked, he continued, "If anyone walks by they'll know you're up here naked, getting punished for not following the rules." He could tell that excited her by the way her legs nearly gave out. Circling his arm around her waist, he anchored her against him, offering his support until she managed to right herself.

He put his mouth close to her ear. "You okay?" he whispered, stepping out of his role momentarily.

She nodded and turned her head to face him. "Better than okay," she murmured softly, and the depth of emotions in her voice took him by surprise. He locked his knees to avoid collapsing. The tender way she looked at him immediately brought them to a deeper lever of intimacy. And in that instant when their gazes connected, something happened between them. Something potent, something powerful, something there was no coming back from. He knew she felt it too. Everything in him reached out to her and it suddenly occurred to him how much he wanted her, and he didn't mean just physically.

He molded his chest to her back and angled her chin, forcing her to look out the window.

"Tell me what you see."

Reaching in front of her, he ran the leather flogger between her legs.

She was barely able to answer as the toy stimulated her sex. "I...I see Candace and Anna coming back."

With a quick flick of his wrist, the leather straps brushed against her pussy and connected with her clit. Her body shook. Uncontrollably.

"Can they see you?" His voice sounded rough and raspy, even to himself.

Lindsay's breath came in a labored burst. "No."

"If you scream they'll see you, Lindsay." Brad drew the flogger back and whacked her ass, testing her restraint, pushing her limits.

"Oh God," she whimpered.

"Be careful. Unless, of course, you want to get caught playing sex games with your handyman."

She shook her head no and he smacked her again. Hard. Her body jutted forward against the windowpane, a low blissful moan rose from her throat.

"Did they hear you that time?"

"No."

"You know they'll come bursting in here to see if you're okay." He whacked again, harder this time, leaving a bright pink spot on her curvy cheek.

She bit back a moan. "I know."

"We wouldn't want that now would we?"

Inching back, he grabbed the nipple clamps and then spun her around to face him. The elated look on her face took his breath away. God, she was the most incredible woman he'd ever met.

He anchored her arms to her sides and attached the clamps to her rosy nipples. A low hiss slipped from her lips. It sounded like a hiss from pain, not pleasure.

Brad froze. His stomach plummeted. Damn, he was hurting her. He hadn't meant to. He hungered to give her what she craved but didn't want to hurt her in the process. He almost dropped the role and cradled her in his arms until she said, "I forgot I wasn't supposed to talk until I had permission. I understand if you must punish me."

He smiled, realizing how well she could read him and how in tune she was with his body language. His tension eased as he understood it was her way of comforting him and assuring him that he had nothing to worry about, that the pain was part of the pleasure. A barrage of emotions overtook him, making it hard to focus.

Something deep inside him compelled him to kiss her, needing the intimate connection more than life itself. Leaning into her, he put his lips over hers, giving her a warm, soulful kiss. He felt her body relax into his, felt the way she gave herself over to him, trusting him completely with her pleasure and her pain.

Brad trailed kisses over her cheek, her neck and her breasts. He sank to his knees and insinuated himself between her legs. With the tips of his fingers he pulled open her soft folds. God he needed to taste her.

"Do you know what I see?"

Her words were fractured. "What...what do you mean?"

He licked her, a long luxurious lick all the way from the back to the front. "I see a strong woman putting her pleasures in my hand, praying that I just might know what she wants." He swirled his tongue over her engorged clit and looked up at her. She raked her fingers through his hair, and when their eyes met, it brought them an even deeper level of intimacy. "And you know what, Lindsay?"

He could tell it took effort for her to talk. "What?" she whispered.

"I do know what you want."

A soft breathless whimper sounded in her throat as he pushed a finger inside her tight channel. His tongue raked over her clit and just like that, she climaxed all over his hand and in his mouth. It amazed him at how her body responded so readily to him.

As he lapped at her creamy essence and absorbed her tremor, he knew beyond a shadow of a doubt, after sampling her sweetness, he'd never have a taste for another.

Chapter Five

Lindsay ran her fingers through Brad's hair as the soft blade of his tongue soothed her swollen clitoris. God, she'd never come so hard or so fast in her entire life, with or without a man. His bold, sexy words, combined with the intimate feel of his fingers deep inside her, stroking her G-spot, had her going off like a Roman candle. Holy hell the man knew just how to touch her and just how to talk to her to drive her into a sexual frenzy.

Brad had quickly brought her to never-before-known heights of excitement with his sexy little bondage games. But the truth was, she wanted more from him, and she wasn't even close to sating her sexual appetite. She suspected when it came to him, she never would be.

Lindsay needed to see him naked so she could touch and kiss and pleasure his rock-hard body, the same exquisite way he'd pleasured hers. She craved the feel of his thick cock inside her, and ached to climb over him and ride him with wild abandon until they both reached earth-shattering climaxes.

Still breathless, she gripped his shoulders. "Come here, Brad."

He slid up her body, removed her nipple clamps with the utmost care and brought his mouth close to hers. It occurred to her that Brad took great care in everything he did, from taking down a wall to giving her an orgasm.

"Hey." He pressed his body to hers. "Are you doing okay?"

She nodded and brushed her lips over his, enjoying the taste of her desire on his mouth.

"Mmmm," he moaned when her tongue slipped inside to play with his. His warm breath wafted across her face and filled her with a longing. She broke the gentle kiss, inched back and looked at him, really looked at him. His expression was warm, tender and vulnerable, and stirred her insides.

She gulped air. Oh God, he had a way of touching her so deeply it made her insides quake. Self-preservation urged her to ignore the emotions he brought out in her and concentrate only on the lust still burning up inside her.

She cupped his cheek and he leaned into her hand. "Thank you," she whispered into his mouth.

He grinned and brushed her bangs from her forehead. "My pleasure."

Her hands left his face, trailed over his hard, muscular chest and went to his trim waist. She tugged his shirt out from his jeans. In her most sultry voice she murmured, "Speaking of your pleasure."

His hand closed over hers and stopped her fingers from exploring further. His eyes were dark and serious, his voice full of tender concern. "I want you, Lindsay, all of you, but don't feel the need to do this if you don't really want to. It gave me pleasure just to pleasure you."

It gave him pleasure just to pleasure her.

Her heart turned over in her chest. So far Brad had proven to be different from any of the guys she'd had relationships with. He was perceptive and smart, caring enough to look beneath her surface to understand her needs and desires. She'd been with men longer, had dated them for months even, and they still hadn't been able to read her the way Brad had. Honestly, no matter how much she craved to be dominated in the bedroom, she wasn't about to come right out and tell a guy she wanted to be spanked or tied up, but Brad could see through her, see her deepest darkest desire.

Oh boy, she was in trouble here.

Because this was just supposed to be about sex. They'd agreed on it.

His hand closed over hers and squeezed, bringing her thoughts back to him. She noted how his tender touch traveled all the way to her heart and caused her chest to ache. It was slight, but none the less, it was still there.

She brushed her hand over his cock, wanting to give him everything he'd given her and more. Wanting to make it as perfect for him as he'd made it for her. Suddenly his pleasure became more important than her very next breath.

"Trust me, Brad. I have to do this. This is about my pleasure too." She gave him a smile.

The rough pad of his thumb scraped over her mouth, his eyes glazed with lust and anticipation. "Well if you insist."

"Oh I insist." She slipped her hand inside his pants and connected with his engorged shaft. His groan reverberated through her body.

She sheathed his thickness in her palm and squeezed. Lord, his cock was the best thing she'd ever felt. Long, smooth and hard. For her. Her mouth salivated, eager for a deep, thorough taste.

Lindsay kissed him on the mouth and then pushed him backwards until his knees hit the mattress. She waved her finger at him and gave him a mischievous smile. "Take off your pants."

He tore open the zipper, pulled them off and kicked them aside, all in record time.

"Good. Now the shirt." That disappeared just as fast.

Lindsay took a long moment to admire his gorgeous, naked, bronzed body. Reluctantly, she tore her gaze away, letting it drift to the cardboard box in the corner. Her mind raced as she mentally catalogued the contents.

Brad shot her a nervous glance and swiped his bangs to the side. She could see perspiration dotting his flesh. "Lindsay? I'm not—"

"Shh." She silenced him with her fingertips. "I don't remember giving you permission to talk," she teased.

When he frowned, her heart went out to him. The poor guy had no idea how much he was going to enjoy this.

She touched his cheek and softened her voice. "You have to trust me, Brad. Trust that I know you'll enjoy this. The same way I trusted you."

His brow smoothed out, his eyes relaxed and he gave a quick nod. "You really are something else, Lindsay. I'm discovering you're a lot different from the women I'm used to."

She frowned and planted her hands on her hips. "Different? As in deviant sex-crazed-woman-who-likes-to-be-spanked different?"

He chuckled. "Well, when you put it that way."

"Hey," she said wagging a warning finger at him. "Play nice."

He gave her the devil's grin. "I always play nice, Lindsay. I thought you'd know that by now." When she cast him a skeptical glance, he put his hand to his chest. "I meant it as a compliment, scout's honor."

"Well alright then." She tossed him a grin and spun

around.

Before she could make her way to the box, Brad cupped her elbow, turned her around and urged her back. As their bodies collided, he brushed his thumb over her bottom lip and pulled her impossibly close. The feel of his thick cock pressing against her stomach drew her attention and made her shiver in anticipation.

His voice dropped an octave. "I really like that you feel comfortable enough with me to just let go and be yourself. And I like what we did, Lindsay. I really, really liked it."

"Yeah?"

"Yeah," he assured her. "I never knew sex games could be so much fun. Thanks for showing me."

There was that tenderness and vulnerability in his eyes again. Lindsay nodded, unable to find her voice. Fighting down the barrage of emotions, she twisted around and made her way to the box. She pulled out the honey dust, a feather and a squeezable bottle of peach-flavored Hot Kisses. Brad looked like the kind of guy who'd appreciate peach flavor, which just so happened to be her favorite.

She gathered her supplies in a pile and made her way back to Brad. Body hard, cock aching, he stood there, gaze riveted, silently watching her with hungry eyes. Her body immediately grew needy for him again.

She stood in front of him. His warm familiar scent curled around her, arousing all her senses. With a slight nudge she pushed him onto the bed. His large frame hit with a thud. Once again, Lindsay spent a moment just staring at him, unable to believe this gorgeous specimen was hers to do with as she wished. And boy, oh boy, did she have a lot of wishes.

She dropped her goodies onto the nightstand and climbed over him, her long legs straddling his waist. His thick cock pressed against her ass and felt so damn incredible. It almost made her abandon her plan to drive him into a sexual frenzy, the same way he had done to her, and just climb on board for the ride of her life.

Brad gripped her hips and ground his cock into her backside. "Jesus, Lindsay, you've got me so hard, I'm going to erupt."

Resisting the urge to impale herself on him, Lindsay gyrated her body, enjoying the way it stimulated her oversensitive clit. A moment later, she slid off his lap. There were things she wanted to do to him first before he *erupted*. She grabbed her feather and lightly brushed it over his throbbing cock. Brad put his hands over his head and groaned. "Are you trying to kill me?"

She opened the bottle of peach honey dust, dipped the feather in. In one fluid movement, she brushed it over his cock, like she was painting a masterpiece. Once she was satisfied she'd covered every square inch, she put the feather aside. "Perfect," she said, pleased with her work.

Brad made a deep guttural sound and she could almost feel the sexual frustration grip him. "Perfect? No, not perfect. You're killing me."

With that, Lindsay settled herself on her knees, bent forward and sank his engorged cock to the back of her throat, enjoying the delicious taste of peach mingling with the arousing taste of Brad's liquid heat.

Suddenly, Brad's growl segued into a low heated moan. His hips jerked forward, his fingers tangled through her long curls, pulling her hair off her face so he could see her slick mouth in action.

"Okay, now that is perfect," he managed to force out between deep raspy groans.

Obviously Brad had a few fetishes of his own.

Knowing he was watching, she wanted him to enjoy the show. "Mmmm..." she moaned, moving her head up and down as her other hand slipped underneath to cradle his balls. His cock swelled in her mouth, the veins filling with heated blood. After a long moment of tasting him, she inched back and began to work her tongue over his shaft, taking time to swirl around the tip and lick underneath his bulbous head.

She felt his fingers tighten in her hair and knew he wasn't kidding when he said he was ready to erupt. She nipped at him, easing off a bit, giving him reprieve.

Her tongue found his stomach, she licked a path back up to his mouth. "How you doing?" She put all her weight on top of him, loving the way he felt beneath her, loving the way her heavy, swollen breasts pressed into his chest. She rubbed against him, her nipples quivering in delight.

He grabbed her hands and threaded his fingers through hers. His muscles were tight, pumped. His eyes were dark with desire, his gaze was probing, deep. "I want to fuck you, Lindsay."

She leaned into him and slid her tongue over his bare skin, reveling in his salty taste. Her voice was whispery soft. "I want to fuck you too, Brad, but not just yet. There is one more thing I want to do for you, if you think you're up to it."

He jerked his hips forward, driving his cock against her. Humor edged his voice. "I believe I'm up for anything."

His head lifted, his mouth connected with hers. After a thorough taste, he pulled back and licked his lips. "Peach. My favorite. How'd you know?"

She rolled her shoulder. "It appears that we both seem to know a lot about each other, now doesn't it?"

He smiled. "Appears so."

Lindsay turned her attention to the bottle of Hot Kisses. She gave it a light shake. "This you are going to love."

All humor disappeared from his voice, not even a trace remained. "Show me," he said—an invitation to experiment, which she had every intention of doing.

She dipped her finger into the Hot Kisses and lathered it onto his cock. Stroking her hand up and down in a slow seduction.

He flinched. "Fuck, that's cold."

"Give it a second." Lindsay continued to rub until he was well coated, then she leaned forward and blew a hot breath on his throbbing cock.

She could hear the breath rush from his lungs. "Jesus Christ, Lindsay, what the hell is that stuff?"

She chuckled and blew again. "It has heating properties in it that are activated by blowing."

"It's so hot. I've never felt anything like it."

Another warm breath had his body shaking, she could see his juices drip from the slit and knew he was teetering on the edge, one more blow would send him sailing over.

His voice came out hard. "My pants. Back pocket. Wallet. Condom. Now."

The dark passion in his tones frightened and excited her at once. Lindsay jumped from the bed, found the condom, ripped it open and quickly sheathed him. Brad grabbed her, pulled her onto the bed beside him and rolled on top of her. "I need to fuck you."

Lindsay drew a quick sharp breath, her entire body going up in a ball of flames. "Yes, I think that's a good idea."

He looked frenzied, uncontrolled. In one quick thrust Brad entered her. He adjusted his arms to keep most of his body weight from crushing her as his thick cock pushed open the tight walls of her pussy.

"Oh God," Lindsay cried out, her legs going around his back, her fingers digging into his flesh, holding him to her, never wanting to let him go.

He plunged into her harder and harder, going impossibly deeper. She met each thrust with one of her own. Sweat collected on their bodies as they joined as one, both taking and giving what they needed.

He gripped one of her legs and put it around his shoulder, angling her for an even deeper thrust.

She gulped air, unable to fill her lungs to their fullest. "I'm—" Her body exploded into a million tiny fragments before she had time to finish the sentence. Her sex muscles quaked and throbbed as Brad brought on her second orgasm.

"I know, babe, me too," and with that, he threw his head back and groaned, his cock pulsing and jerking as he gave himself over to his climax.

A moment later Brad rolled beside her, their bodies sated and drained from their incredible sex. And incredible was definitely the term she'd use to describe it.

Brad snuggled her in next to him, his tender gaze met hers. "Hey, babe."

Oh God, she'd never felt so close, so connected to anyone before. She worked to find her voice. "Hey yourself," she said as his heat wrapped around her like a silken cocoon. His lips found hers and gave her a slow, gentle kiss, one that stirred all her emotions.

"You are incredible," he breathed into her mouth.

She raked his hair from his forehead and drew a fortifying breath. "You're not so bad yourself."

As she gazed into his eyes, her heart went to her throat. It occurred to her that bad-boy Brad Caldwell had definitely helped tamp down the fire in her body, but in the process, he'd left behind his warmth.

Chapter Six

Two birds chirping a love song outside the window of the inn pulled Lindsay from her slumber. She stretched out her body, a contented smile on her mouth, and realized she'd never felt so sexually satisfied in her entire life.

She slid her hand across the huge bed and, much to her dismay, found the space empty, cold. After their amazing love-making session the night before, Brad had told her he had to leave, that he had responsibilities to take care of, responsibilities that couldn't be neglected.

That made her wonder, and worry. The truth was she didn't really know a lot about him. She was pleased to meet a man who had responsibilities, and who took them seriously. Meeting a man like that was a rarity for her. In fact, a lot of things about Brad were a rarity.

But what responsibilities was he talking about? Did he have a woman somewhere waiting for him? That thought made her stomach tighten and palms sweat. Or did he simply get what he wanted from her and take off, like the other men she knew? Then again, it's not like she could blame him. She *had* assured him it was just about sex.

As her thoughts raced, it occurred to her just how much she liked him. How possessive she felt of him.

So much for sex easing the tremendous tension between

them. Not only did it make her want him more, it created a whole new set of problems for her.

Disgruntled with the direction of her thoughts, Lindsay climbed from the bed and scooped yesterday's clothes off the wooden floor. She needed to put Brad out of her head and get her focus back on to matters at hand. After all she'd told him she was only in it for the sex, and apparently he didn't have any qualms about that.

So sex it was, and sex is all it would be.

Her tummy grumbled, reminding her she hadn't eaten since breakfast the previous day. She'd skipped lunch with the girls when her equipment had arrived, and she'd skipped dinner because she and Brad had been too busy playing sex games to stop for nourishment.

Lindsay pulled her clothes on and padded barefoot to her door. She quietly eased it open and peeked out, wondering what her friends would think if they knew she'd spent all of yesterday having sex with Brad. Hadn't they all made a vow to swear off men? Lord, she'd only made it two months. Libidinous slut that she was. Then again, how could she possibly resist a man like Brad, one who was so caring, so considerate, one who touched her with such tender care and was so damn in tune with her needs and desires?

She tiptoed into the hall and listened for her friends. Candace's door was shut, so was Anna's. She wondered for a moment if they too had worked late into the night and stayed over, or if they had made their way home.

As she pondered it a minute longer, the delicious scent of apple muffins caught her attention. Yummy.

After freshening up in the bathroom, Lindsay made her way into the kitchen. There she found Pamina talking to her cat. What a strange lady she was. The woman was far too young and beautiful to be one of those crazy cat ladies. That future, undoubtedly, was reserved for Lindsay.

Pamina twisted around to greet her, a bright smile lighting up her gorgeous eyes. Her voice as cheerful as ever, she said, "Good morning, Lindsay."

"Good morning, Pamina, Abra."

Abra jumped from Pamina's arms and curled around her legs. Pamina chuckled and shook her head. "It appears that Abra is enjoying your company, Lindsay. He seems to have an affinity for Candace and Anna too. I saw him saunter out of Candace's room this morning as a matter of fact." She tossed Abra a scolding look. "He might be an old *Tom* cat but he's not supposed to be a *peeping* Tom cat."

Lindsay thought the comment odd, but chose to ignore it. Instead she arched a questioning brow. "Candace spent the night?" Her mind raced, wondering if Candace had heard the commotion going on in her room. Then again, if she recalled correctly she did hear a lot of banging coming from down that end of the hall. She made a note to check in with both her girls later.

"Is Candace feeling okay? She looked a little flushed yesterday."

Pamina grinned and made her way to the oven. "She's perfectly fine."

Lindsay opened her mouth to ask about Anna, but Pamina answered her unasked question. "Both girls are perfectly fine and their rooms are coming along splendidly." Pamina stepped up to the table with a dozen muffins. She pushed her fruit bowl to the side, turned the tray upside down and plopped the muffins onto a plate.

Lindsay helped herself. She inhaled the delicious aroma and bit into the scrumptious treat. "What's with you and apples anyway?"

Pamina waved her hand toward the backyard. "One should never waste nature's gift."

Lindsay followed her gaze until her eyes settled on a huge tree, its branches heavy with crisp red apples. "I don't remember that being there."

"That's because you've not taken the time to explore the grounds. There is a beautiful pond out back as well. A great place for lovers to sit and chat, don't you think?"

At the mere mention of lovers, Lindsay's mind reeled. She wanted to ask Pamina about Brad, but she didn't want to sound too obvious. Once again, as though Pamina could read her mind, she directed the conversation.

"Brad is doing a wonderful job."

Her body warmed all over. Good Lord, just the mention of his name had her going all weird inside.

Lindsay tried for casual but suspected Pamina, being as perceptive as she was, could see right through her. "Yeah, he should be done by tonight." Her stomach plummeted, knowing it would be the last she'd see of him.

"And then he will be gone and you'll be able to finish up your room. You must be thrilled about that, Lindsay?"

Thrilled wasn't the word she'd use. Lindsay nodded and bit into her breakfast, even though she no longer had an appetite.

"How do you know him?" she asked, deciding to come right out and pry.

Pamina grabbed her own muffin and placed it on a napkin. "I don't."

That surprised Lindsay. Somehow she'd thought they knew each other. "Oh, then why did you hire him?"

"I found his name in the phone book. I heard good things

about his business. And I didn't hire him, you did."

Lindsay wiped crumbs from her mouth. "When he left yesterday he said he had responsibilities. I guess he must have had other jobs to take care of."

"I suppose that's possible. Brad has proven to be quite the hard worker."

Lindsay agreed. "Yeah, different from the men I know."

"But I do wonder why he agreed to take a job so far from home. Don't you?"

Lindsay narrowed her brow and pursed her lips in thought. She'd been wondering that herself. Brad had said no job was too small, but she didn't buy that for a minute. There was more going on with him than he let on.

"Why don't you ask him?"

Lindsay's head came up, her eyes narrowed. How did Pamina always know what she was thinking? "What?"

"Ask him what responsibilities took him away. I'm sure it must have been important. Otherwise why would he rush away, especially when things were going so good for him here?" Pamina winked at her and offered her a fresh, juicy peach from the fruit bowl.

Lindsay choked on her muffin. Good Lord, did the woman know all her secrets?

Suddenly, she went warm all over. And she knew there was only one reason for that. Brad was here. She felt his presence even before she saw him. Everything in her body tingled just knowing he was in close proximity.

"Good morning, ladies."

Lindsay dropped her muffin and turned to face him. When she spotted him standing in the doorway, her body buzzed to life. She took in the warm look in his eyes as they met hers, and her heart turned over in her chest. She fought down a barrage of emotions, reminding herself that what was between them was sex. Damn great sex, mind you. And nothing more.

She took a moment to peruse him. Dressed in a pair of jeans and a snug T-shirt that hugged his body to perfection, he had *morning after* written all over him. She swallowed and admired his shaved face. His thick hair looked damp, from a recent shower. God she loved how he pushed his bangs to the side. It made him look so damn sexy.

With effort, she said, "You're here early." Did she dare hope it was because he couldn't wait to go another round with her?

"I thought I'd get at the room right away so you can start your painting. I know how anxious you are to put the room together."

Damn. She forced a smile. "I see."

Silence reigned heavy as they both stared at one another, sexual sparks arcing between them. After a long moment, Pamina spoke. "Well, head right on up, Brad. The sooner you get started, the sooner you finish. I'm sure you must have other, more pressing jobs waiting for you."

Brad nodded and disappeared down the hall, and Lindsay resisted the urge to follow, peach in hand.

The morning had flown by rather quickly as Lindsay sorted through numerous paint chips until she got the exact color she had in mind.

Sitting at the kitchen table, she kept glancing into the hall. She hadn't seen Brad all morning, leaving him alone to finish his job so he could get on to more pressing matters.

Like spanking her again. Good Lord.

Come to think of it, Candace or Anna hadn't surfaced

either. She'd gone to check on them earlier, but their doors were locked. She hadn't wanted to knock and wake them in case they'd been up all night working.

It was nearing lunch, and her tummy grumbled. Maybe now was a good time to check on Brad, to see if he needed a sandwich or to see if he wanted to go another round on her padded bench. Her thighs trembled just thinking about it.

Lindsay quietly made her way upstairs. She peeked into her room. "Brad, I thought you might like a sand—" Her words fell off when she looked around and found the room empty. Three steps took her to the window. She glanced out and spotted his truck in the driveway, but he was nowhere to be found.

She also noticed two other trucks parked on the street. Had Candace and Anna hired someone too? Dear God, perhaps they were up to the same thing as she was.

Before she had time to investigate, Pamina stepped into the room with a picnic basket. "I thought you might like to sit out at the pond and have lunch."

Lindsay smiled. Just then her stomach grumbled louder. "I'd love to."

They descended the stairs, walked out the back door and made their way to the apple tree. Lindsay tightened her sweater around her, breathed in the crisp autumn air and admired the beautiful colors on the fall foliage. "It's just gorgeous out here." She angled her head to see Pamina. "Like you said earlier, a wonderful place for lovers."

Pamina handed her the picnic basket.

Lindsay frowned. "Aren't you—?"

"Like I said, Lindsay, a wonderful place for lovers." She waved her hand and Lindsay followed the direction. Her heart leapt when she spotted Brad sitting by the lake, legs crossed, head down, as though deep in thought.

"Enjoy." Pamina then disappeared.

Lindsay drew a centering breath and with a lighthearted bounce to her step made her way to Brad.

She cleared her throat, heralding her arrival. "Hey," she said as she came up beside him. It occurred to her that he'd been so engrossed in some book he hadn't even heard her approach.

Startled, he closed the book on his lap and tucked it in beside him, out of her view.

How odd.

"Hey yourself." He gave her a sexy smile that warmed her right down to her toes. "What are you doing out here?"

"Taking a break, like you." She produced the basket. "I thought we could have lunch."

He patted the ground beside him and she quickly took her seat. She gestured with her head. "What are you reading?"

"Nothing."

"Obviously it's not nothing." She reached across him and grabbed the book. When she read the title she was taken aback. She glanced at him, her eyes questioning. "What's this?"

He snatched the book back and put it inside his backpack. "Like I said, nothing."

"You're studying for a medical entrance exam?" Wow, there was a whole lot more to this guy than she knew.

He rolled one shoulder, brushing it off. "Yeah." In an attempt to change the conversation, he reached for the basket. "What did you bring?"

She wasn't about to let him off so easily. "When we were chatting about your job, about being a handyman, how come you didn't tell me?"

His eyes got serious for a moment. "Most people think it's ridiculous."

As he reached into the basket, she said, "Well I don't. You certainly have the brains for it."

His hands stopped, and he looked at her. "What makes you say that?"

"You run your own business, don't you, and you can put up walls as well as tear them down." Not to mention that he was smart enough to understand her needs and desires in the bedroom, unlike the other men she'd been with. "Stupid people can't do that."

He laughed and squeezed her leg. "You're so politically incorrect, Lindsay."

She offered him a wry smile and grabbed an egg-salad sandwich. She bit into it and chewed, letting the information sink in. "So you want to be a doctor." It was a statement, not a question.

"Yup," he said between bites. "My secret's out."

"I think that is fabulous."

His head came up. "Really? You do?"

"Sure I do. Of course I never thought there was anything wrong with being a handyman, but being a doctor rocks too."

He gave her a genuine smile and her insides turned to meringue. Oh boy. She had it bad for him.

She winked. "Hey, do you need any help studying? I could go over the male anatomy section with you if you'd like."

Brad laughed out loud. "You really are something else, Lindsay. Quite different from any other woman I've met."

She rolled her eyes. "I know, I know, we've been over that already." She squinted and studied him for a minute. "Seriously though, Brad, how come you never mentioned it when we were chatting? How come you kept it a secret?"

He shrugged. "Like I said, most people laugh. No one has ever supported my dream. Even though I've got a science degree behind me, most people don't think I'm going to do anything with it, and that I'm going to stay a handyman forever. They figure I'm great to have sex with and nothing more," he admitted honestly.

She suspected it took a considerable amount of trust on his part to tell her something so personal. She suddenly recalled their conversation, just before they had sex. Her stomach lurched remembering how she told him there could only be sex between them, proving she was no different from any other woman he'd been with. "Well, I wouldn't laugh. I think it's wonderful, Brad."

He leaned back on his elbows. His voice was low, soft, barely audible. "Thank you."

It suddenly occurred to her why he'd come all the way to Mason Creek to work. "I'm guessing you took this job way out of town to make extra money to help pay for MCAT prep classes."

"Pretty perceptive, aren't you?"

"Yes, I pride myself on that," she teased. "So tell me, do you have enough money?" Not that it was any of her business, but she really wanted to know. It mattered to her. He mattered to her.

He shook his head and she could tell he wasn't all that comfortable talking money with her. She narrowed her eyes and studied him. There were fine lines around his eyes and she wondered for a minute if he even slept last night.

"Did you get any sleep after you left here?"

"No, I had another job to go to. The pay was too good to turn down."

"Can you ask your family to help?"

"My dad died when I was in high school, and mom is sick. So with her expenses, and taking care of my two younger siblings, I don't think I'm going to take the prep classes this year. I'm still a couple thousand short." She could hear the sincerity, the love and the responsibility in his voice.

Mind sorting through everything, Lindsay leaned in next to his warm body and snuggled in tight. He turned until they were face to face, chest to chest and hip to hip. He touched her cheek and in no time at all, desire overtook them. Their lips met in a frenzied kiss and in that instant she knew she wanted more from him. He was everything she'd ever wanted in a man, and she had no doubt that she wanted something a little more permanent.

God, she'd told him this was just about sex, but in the span of a few short hours, things had changed for her. She cared for him. A lot. And she needed to show him how much. She knew of only one way to do that. By showing support where others hadn't. She was going to do something she'd sworn she'd never, ever do again.

Chapter Seven

Less than two hours later, Brad had Lindsay's room all cleaned up. He'd swept, cleared out all his supplies and had taken the plaster to the dump for disposal.

Now that his job was completed, he needed to talk to Lindsay, to tell her how he felt. To see if she wanted to explore their relationship further and see where it led. Like he hoped she did.

He stood back and admired the wide open space. Lindsay's voice gained his attention. Just her sultry tone alone had his body reacting with heated anticipation. Desire twisted inside him as she stepped closer.

"It looks fabulous, Brad. It really opens the room up."

He turned to face her and smiled at the endorsement. "Thanks."

He held his arms out to her and she moved into them. He wove his fingers through hers and tugged until their bodies collided. God, her heat scorched him and made him wild with need. He brushed a wayward chestnut lock from her face and put his mouth close to her ear.

"Lindsay, we need to talk." As soon as the words left his mouth, he mentally kicked himself. He hadn't meant to approach her that way. He knew firsthand that those words were usually the kiss of death. He'd heard them himself a time or two, women letting him know they wanted sex, not emotional commitment from him.

She removed herself from the circle of his arms and stepped back, her lips thinned to a fine line. Her voice tight, edgy. "Brad, wait."

Everything in him reached out to her. Damn she must have read him wrong, either that or she was about to give him the brush-off. Shit, either way, this wasn't good. "Lindsay—"

She held an envelope out to him. "I want you to have this."

"What is it?"

Looking a bit unsettled, she shoved it at him. "Just take it, please."

"What's going on, Lindsay?" As he read her body language, his gut churned, he had a bad feeling. Her face was anxious, her stance antsy. Brad accepted the envelope and ripped it open. When he peered inside, his stomach hit the ground like a felled wall.

Jesus H. Christ.

Nausea welled up inside him but quickly segued to anger. Pride crushed, he'd never been so offended in his entire fucking life.

"What the—"

Lindsay rushed out, "I want you to keep it."

He stepped back, hands curling and uncurling as anger swept through his bloodstream until he saw red. After the intimacies they'd shared, after talking and getting to know each other on another level, how could she turn around and do something like this?

What made her think he was the kind of guy who would take money from her? Goddammit. And what the fuck was it for, services rendered? Lord, he'd never felt so used, so prostituted in his life.

"You can use it for your prep course."

Jesus, did he seem that shallow? That he'd mooch off her. "Are you fucking kidding me?"

Her eyes narrowed, confused.

"Lindsay, Christ." He stumbled over his words and took a distancing step backwards. It felt like she was paying him off. To leave nicely. A thank-you for the good times. Wham, bam, thank you, handyman.

Incredulous, he looked at her for a long moment and then tossed the money onto the bench. The same bench where he'd made love to her and *thought* they'd made an emotional connection.

"Keep your money. My services were free."

Before she had time to speak, he shoved the door open. It hit the wall with a thud and nearly ripped off its hinges. He stormed out the door and, without so much as a backward glance, flew down the staircase. Too bad his heart hadn't come with him.

The sound of his heavy work boots reverberated through the hallway as he hastily sailed through the house and made his way to his truck. He shoved the key into the ignition, but the goddamned thing wouldn't turn over.

"Now what," he said, slamming his hand on the steering wheel. He pushed his door open and climbed from the driver's seat. After popping the hood, he examined his battery.

"Having trouble, Brad?"

He angled his head to see Pamina behind him. He didn't have time for this, not when he just wanted to get the fuck out of Dodge.

"It won't turn over," he bit out and immediately berated

himself for snapping. Pamina wasn't the one he was angry with and he had no right to take it out on her. The truth was, he was pissed with Lindsay and with himself. Pissed with her because she didn't want more from him, and pissed with himself because he'd allowed himself to believe there was a possibility she would. When the fuck would he learn that women wanted him for a good romp and nothing else?

She touched his arm, and he turned to face her. "Do you love her?"

At first that question took him by surprise, but then it occurred to him his actions were pretty transparent. "It doesn't matter."

"I can't blame you for loving her. She's a very special girl."

He narrowed his gaze, wondering where this was heading.

"I guess it makes one curious why such a special girl like her is still single."

That thought had crossed his mind a time or two, or a thousand.

She lowered her voice. "Well between us, Brad, Lindsay has sworn off men. She doesn't want anything more to do with relationships."

His stomach clenched. Fuck, he already knew Lindsay was just in it for the ride, he didn't need Pamina reminding him.

Pamina tsked and shook her head. "Such a shame, really. It seems that all the men in her life had been eager to mooch off her, eager to separate her from her money. A few months back, she'd had enough of it and had given up on the opposite sex."

His mind raced, remembering their conversation over lunch. Him telling her he needed money for his exams. Obviously she thought he was looking for something from her, the same way every other man had. But after everything they shared, he thought she'd have known him better than that, thought she'd seen him as something different.

"I guess it would take a pretty special guy to get her to trust again. And if she ever offered a man money, it would merely be her way of showing she trusted, she cared. It'd be a big leap of faith on her part, don't you think?"

Brad stilled. Oh shit. He hadn't seen that coming.

Numb and a bit confused, Lindsay watched him go. *Okay,* that hadn't gone quite as planned.

Just then Candace and Anna came racing in from their rooms. Candace reached her first. "What's going on? I heard a bang? Are you okay?"

Stomach in knots, Lindsay said, "I don't think so."

Anna wrapped her arms around her waist. "You're so pale." She touched Lindsay's forehead. "Are you sick?"

When she shook her head, Candace and Anna exchanged a worried look.

With kid gloves, Anna walked her toward the door, Candace tight on their heels. "Come on, let's get you some water."

They led her to the kitchen and once she was seated with a glass of ice water in front of her, Candace plunked down in the chair beside her. "What's going on?"

She wrung her hands together. "I just gave Brad a shitload of money."

Anna pulled a chair up beside her and kept her tone soft. "Are you kidding me, Lindsay?"

"Afraid not."

"Holy shit! Why did you do that?" Candace asked, eyes wide in total shock.

She shrugged. "He needed the money."

Candace threw her head back in disbelief. "So once again a guy has managed to schmooze you and separate you from your money."

Anna cut Candace a stern glance. "Don't be so hard on her."

Candace ignored Anna. "So now that he's got your money, he's gone, right? Good Lord, when are you going to learn the kinds of guys you attract are lazy bastards who simply want to mooch off you."

"Don't talk about him like that, Candace. He's not like other guys. He's a hard worker and he takes care of his family." She lowered her voice. "He's really wonderful. And he didn't even take the money."

"Oh boy," Anna piped in.

Lindsay and Candace turned to face her. "What?" they said in unison.

"Lindsay, do you realize what you're doing?" Anna asked.

"What?"

"You're protecting and supporting him. The same way you always protect and support me and Candace. You only do that with the ones you love."

Oh God, she loved him. She really and truly loved him. And now her goddamn plan to show him just how much she cared had backfired.

"Did you tell him how you felt?" Candace asked.

"I told him I only wanted sex. He agreed."

Candace shook her head in confusion. "So you gave him money?"

"He told me no one had ever supported his dream. I figured if I gave him money it would *show* him how much I cared. Show him that what was between us wasn't just about sex for me, like I had originally said."

Anna softened her voice. "Has he ever told you he felt differently?"

"No, why would he? He went into this thinking of me only as a playmate. And after talking with him, intimately, I now know he's used to that type of behavior from women. He doesn't expect anything more. That's why I felt I needed to show him, and not just tell him."

Brad's voice sounded in the doorway. He pointed to Lindsay. "You. In your bedroom. Now."

Lindsay stood on shaky legs and, as though fearing she was going to bolt, Brad cupped her elbow, packaged her tight against his body and escorted her up the stairs. When they reached the bedroom, she twisted to face him.

"Brad, I..."

He pressed his fingers to her lips. When his eyes met hers, a shiver traveled all the way to her toes. "I'm an idiot." His voice was low, harsh.

Before she had a chance to respond, his mouth smashed down on hers. Hard. His kiss was so full of urgency, need and passion, her body responded in kind. Blood racing, she kissed him back with all the love inside her.

"I'm sorry," she whispered into his mouth, her voice rough with emotion.

Bodies still molded together, Brad inched his mouth back. He cupped her cheeks and held her face between his palms. God, she loved how he touched her in such a familiar way. She arched into him and when she saw love shining in his eyes, her heart slammed in her chest.

"You don't have anything to be sorry about." The heat of his breath assailed her neck and aroused all her senses. Her skin came alive with desire.

She worked to find her voice and slid her tongue over her bottom lip. "When I offered you that money, I didn't stop to think it would offend you. Or make you feel used, the way other women have made you feel. It was just my way of showing I cared, where no one else did."

His hands were all over her, like he couldn't get enough. "I know that now, Lindsay. I should have trusted that it was a heartfelt gesture, that you were doing it because you cared."

"Old insecurities are hard to let go of, Brad. I know that firsthand."

"Fortunately Pamina helped me understand things."

Lindsay's fingers raced through his hair, pulling him impossibly closer to her. "Pamina?"

She could feel his body trembling with pent-up need. "Yeah, she explained to me how men always used you and how offering me money was a big leap of faith on your part."

Lindsay furrowed her brow. "I don't know how that woman knows so much." But none of that really mattered to her right now, because standing before her was the man of her dreams and the look on his face told her all she needed to know. He loved her as much as she loved him.

Brad slipped his hands to the small of her back and splayed them open. She watched his throat as he swallowed. His voice dropped to a whisper and there was such tenderness in his gaze. "Before you I never believed in love at first sight."

"Me neither."

"I love you, Lindsay, and I'm never going to let you slip away."

She grinned, her heart nearly exploding in her chest. "I love you too, Brad. But just how do you plan on doing that?"

Mischief filled his eyes. "I do have my ways," he assured her, his glance going to the goodie box.

"Show me," she said, inviting him to answer the pull between her legs.

"It'd be my pleasure."

She smiled. "I'm pretty sure it would be my pleasure too."

He furrowed his brow, his voice taking on a hard edge. "I'm sorry, did you somehow think I gave you permission to talk?"

Lindsay bit back a smile, thrilled with the way he so easily slipped into his role, a role he played just for her. She'd never met anyone so in tune with her needs, her desires or her emotions before. God she loved him so much she ached.

She assumed her role. "I should probably be punished."

Brad stepped back and let his gaze pan over her body. "Take off your clothes but leave on your panties and bra."

She obliged without hesitation, thankful that she'd put panties on that morning.

Her entire body shook as she watched the way his eyes devoured her with hunger, with heat. Once she was naked, he gripped her hips and backed her up until she was next to the window again. He went to the box and pulled out a set of leather straps.

Oh. Good. God.

With predatory moves he stalked toward her, gripped her wrists and wrapped the straps around them.

"Spread your arms."

Brad shackled her wrists and tied her arms to the hooks meant for the curtain tiebacks, prohibiting her from moving. Such ingenuity. Her body quaked in anticipation, certain she'd never been so excited in her entire life.

His hand stroked over her body, a slow seduction that nearly unhinged her. He caressed the pattern of her curves and then casually made his way downward to her panties. He pressed his finger into her heat and moaned.

"You're very wet, Lindsay."

He was testing her to see if she'd speak, knowing if she did punishment would come. Hell, who was she too disappoint him?

Her mouth curved invitingly. "You make me this way."

He silenced her words with a kiss and inched back. His eyes darkened with passion. His gaze dropped from her eyes, to her lips, to the damp triangular patch between her thighs. He gripped the thin white lace of her panties and, with a light tug, stripped them from her hips.

"Oh my," she whispered, her head falling to the side.

He tsked and shook his head. "Such disobedience. I believe a tongue lashing is in order." He dropped to his knees and put his mouth close to her pussy. His nose nudged her clit, drawing it out from its fleshy hood. He inhaled her scent before licking her lightly.

"Jesus," he growled. "You taste sweeter than a peach."

Lindsay bit down on her bottom lip to suppress a sexually frustrated moan. A shiver prowled through her. "Please," she begged, her body reacting to the lust in his voice.

His rough tongue touched her lips and spread them wide apart. "Open your legs," he demanded.

Lindsay spanned them as far apart as possible. Her entire body lubricated. Warm liquid touched her thighs and made them quake. Heat crawled over her body and warmed her from the inside out.

"So perfect." The warmth from his breath caressed her flesh

and stroked her clit. Her entire body shuddered and she jerked her hips forward, pushing her pussy against his face, begging for more, begging for him to ravish her.

His hand came around to smack her ass. "You're not ready for me yet," he bit out.

Oh God, that slap did the most amazing things to her nerve endings.

His thumb touched her clit, applying gentle pressure. The sweet torture made her convulse. When she wiggled, he smacked her again. "Keep still, Lindsay, or there will be no pleasure for you." The heat in his voice excited her even more.

She whimpered and almost lost it right then and there. She loved how he took control, of her pain and her pleasure.

When he turned his attention to her pussy and dipped his tongue inside, she knew she wouldn't last long.

Brad reached inside the box again and pulled out the bottle of peach-flavored Hot Kisses. He gave it a slight shake and opened it. With a wicked grin on his face, he dipped his finger into liquid and dabbed it on her clit.

The minute the cold touched her heated flesh, she felt all her composure slip away. Brad rubbed, until she was sufficiently coated. Then he pulled her swollen lips apart and blew a cool breath. Her clit tingled, her sex quaked, her world turned upside down. Palming her curves, he held her and absorbed her tremor. Once she stopped shaking, he blew on her sex, and her entire body went up in a burst of flames.

"It feels so good," she managed between gasps.

One finger slipped inside her. "You're very close, Lindsay."

She made a move to rake her hands through his hair but when her arms were tugged back by the leather restraints, it excited her even more.

Brad pushed another finger inside her. It was a deliciously snug fit. With the tip of his tongue, he went to work on her clit. As his heat seared her aching bud, it became her undoing. Lindsay could feel the pressure building inside her, growing in intensity until her body shuddered and throbbed and splintered into a million pieces. Breath rushed from her lungs, liquid arousal rushed from her sex and her legs nearly gave out.

"Brad," she cried out as her orgasm washed over her.

Brad stayed on his knees for a long time, his tongue licking her sex. "God I love you so much, Lindsay," she heard him whisper from between her legs.

A moment later he climbed to his feet and brought his mouth to hers. She could feel his cock press insistently against her stomach and knew she had to feel him inside her.

She could barely think, barely talk. She forced the words out between labored breaths. "I need you inside me, Brad. I want to make love with you."

He touched her cheek and ran his thumb over her eyes, her nose and her mouth. "I'd like nothing more, Lindsay. But you're not ready for me yet." His hands went to her leather restraints and unleashed her.

Her eyes felt heavy. "What are you doing?"

"Now it's my turn, my way."

With her brains still fuzzy from that powerful orgasm, she couldn't comprehend anything he was saying. Instead of asking, she just blindly followed him to the bed.

She stood there, awaiting instruction. As his gaze washed over her with love, it suddenly occurred to her, no instructions were to come. He was showing her what he wanted and needed.

Warm arms circled her waist, his eyes were filled with such tenderness, everything in her reached out to him.

He put his mouth close to her ear. His silky hair swept over her shoulder and brought on a shiver. "I'm so crazy about you." He eased her onto the bed, stood back and removed his clothes. Lindsay watched with heated interest, enjoying the show.

Without taking his hungry gaze off her, Brad grabbed a condom from his wallet, sheathed himself and slid back onto the bed with her. With the utmost care, he lay on top of her and spread her legs with his knees. He traced the pattern of her face as his mouth found hers. His kiss was deep, emotional.

He inched back and met her gaze. His eyes had softened and gone was all the dominance from earlier. One hand touched her face, heat radiated from his fingertips. "Now you're ready for me."

Shifting his position, he took a long moment just to look at her. Then he eased his thick cock inside her, slowly, giving her only one inch at a time, prolonging her pleasure.

His lips took possession of hers and his kiss touched her in places so deep she thought she'd burn up. His warm familiar scent curled around her as he moved his hips, gently, methodically, giving and taking. She became pliable beneath him, offering herself to him fully, body and soul.

His cock pressed deeper, and his thrusts became more urgent. Deep breaths expanded and collapsed his chest as he rocked against her.

"Oh, babe, you are incredible."

Sex had never, ever been this good for her. And she knew why, because she'd never had sex with a man she loved.

His lovemaking was so slow, so tender that it filled her with love and brought her to the edge in no time at all. Her hands curled around his neck as another orgasm pulled at her. "I'm there."

As his eyes locked on hers, languorous warmth stole

through her. "Me too."

She gave herself over to her orgasm and could feel his cock pulse inside her as he too reached his climax. Corded muscles shifted when he angled her for a deeper thrust. His breath came in a ragged burst and he threw his head back as he emptied himself in her.

Her bottom lip caught between her teeth, her whole body shook in delight and the world around her tilted on its axis. Brad remained inside her for a long time, until their breathing returned to normal. She played with his hair, enjoying the weight of his body on hers.

Rolling onto his side, he dragged her with him and pulled her in close. He touched her cheek and gave her a warm smile.

"Wow," she murmured.

Brad chuckled. "You really are something else, you know that?"

When she offered him a sassy grin, his eyes filled with laughter. "Why yes, I do, Brad. But feel free to keep reminding me of that."

"That's a pretty smart mouth you've got there, Lindsay." His hands moved to her hips, his fingers bit into her flesh. "And you know what I do with smart-mouthed women."

Her eyes lit with intrigue. "No, what?"

"I punish them."

All Worked Up

Dedication

To the Wicked Writers, who give new meaning to the word, "wicked".

Chapter One

Interior designer Candace Steele stood on the cracked and pitted sidewalk fringing the unsightly Victorian inn, which was unquestionably defacing the quaint town of Mason Creek, a small community on the outskirts of Connecticut. As she examined the array of landscapers and painters all milling about in an effort to return the insect-infested yard as well as the paint-chipped cedar shingles to their natural beautiful state, she stretched out her legs in preparation for her habitual early-morning run.

Just because she was on a job, hired by a strange mystical-like woman named Pamina, and was on a tight deadline, it didn't mean she was about to give up her regular exercise routine—partly due to the upcoming fall triathlon and partly because the exercise filled her sex-deprived body with endorphins. Since she and her colleagues, Lindsay and Anna, childhood friends and co-owners of the bustling interior design shop, Styles for Living, had all recently sworn off men, she damn well had to get her "natural high" from somewhere.

Candace lunged forward, preparing her thigh muscles for a strenuous workout. While she stretched, she thought about the job ahead and the fantasy-inspired theme room each designer had been hired to create. Lindsay had gone for a BDSM theme, Anna for sweet romance. Candace, however, drawing on her experience as a competitive runner, had decided to create a fantasy room for those interested in a little marathon sex. Talk about a room doing double duty for the actively inclined.

She lunged again and stretched her legs as she considered the props she'd need for her project. But her thoughts suddenly careened off-track when she caught sight of a stripper—a paint stripper, that is—who nearly turned said legs to mush.

Shirtless and sexy in a pair of running shorts, he turned her way, giving her a frontal view, and she took in his bronzed skin as it glistened with perspiration beneath the early-morning autumn sun. With those sculpted chest muscles, tight abdominals and long strong legs, it was clear to Candace that he had the body of an athlete, a man straight out of her erotic fantasies. As she perused him longer, taking pleasure in his short, almost military-cut hairstyle, firm square jaw, dark eyes and commanding presence, she wondered if he had the stamina to keep up with her on the track.

Or in the bedroom.

Damned if she didn't want to go for a test run with him in her soon-to-be-created fantasy-inspired theme room and find out.

Why was it again she'd sworn off men?

As she pondered that a moment longer, wondering if Lindsay and Anna were also questioning the logic behind their pact, her cell phone rang. She pulled it from her zippered pocket and when she glanced at the display name, every reason she had for renouncing the opposite sex came rushing back to her.

Candace didn't approve of nepotism and believed in making it on her own, which was why she'd pursued a career in design instead of working for her father, Jason Krane, a successful New York movie director who could easily make or break the careers of aspiring actors.

Whereas Lindsay attracted lazy good-for-nothing guys who wanted to separate her from her hard-earned money, Candace attracted the opposite: aggressive, career-driven men who would wine, dine and bed her in an effort to get closer to her father. When some guy seemed too good to be true, he usually was. She'd learned the hard way that men didn't covet her for who she was, but for who she could introduce them to. The last thing she wanted was for her father to give these guys preference over others or to show favoritism simply because they were dating her.

She flipped open her cell phone. "Hi, Dad."

"Candace, this is Olive. Your father asked me to connect to you. One moment please and I'll transfer the call."

As her father's secretary put her through, she stole another glace at the sexy paint stripper and the way he carefully worked his hands over the cedar walls, taking his good old time, laboring slowly, methodically, conscientiously. He was a professional through and through, clearly determined to get the job done right. A warm tingle moved all the way through her body and settled deep between her thighs as she considered the way those large capable hands would feel brushing over her body, Mr. Shirtless taking the utmost care to get *that* particular job done right.

The deep sound of her father's breathless voice came through the line and pulled her from her musings. "Candace, honey, how are you?"

She smiled, giving her father her full concentration. "I'm great. How about you?"

God, it was so good to hear his voice. Even though talking with him made it feel like he was close by, he was far away in New York. Candace had been only a child when her parents had split and she'd moved to Connecticut with her mother. She couldn't remember much about New York or her time with her father, since he'd spent most of his days on the movie set, neglecting his family at home. Oh, granted, he'd given to her in other ways and tried to show his love by showering her with toys and money, but as a child Candace couldn't really understand those gestures and only ever wanted his fatherly attention.

When her father went silent on the other end, Candace shook her head and chuckled. It was no wonder her mother had divorced him some twenty years ago. For as long as she'd known him, he'd never given anyone his undivided attention if it didn't directly affect his latest movie. This lack of regard had undoubtedly been the downfall of his marriage. She knew as a director his mind was always in two places at once. As she grew up and entered adulthood, Candace had accepted his absent-minded professor disposition and learned to live with it.

"Dad, are you there?"

"Yes, honey, what is it I can do for you?"

She exhaled an exasperated breath. "You were the one who called me."

"Oh right. Have you read today's paper?"

Disheartened at the way the media always distorted information and cold-heartedly attacked the rich and famous for the sheer pleasure of it, she plunked herself down on the sunburnt grass and blew a heavy sigh. "Yeah, I read it."

Her father went silent for a moment. She listened to the sound of papers rustling in the background. "It's not true," he piped up.

"I know. You don't have to call me every time, Dad. I know the accusations aren't true and you didn't fire Ginger Simone because she wouldn't sleep with you." He'd fired her because during the first week of shooting she never bothered to show up to the set. That woman was a prima donna through and through. Just then Lindsay, Anna, Pamina—along with Pamina's fat cat, Abra—came sauntering out of the house. Candace gave them a wave and they all shouted a greeting as they walked to the masonry truck that had suddenly materialized in the driveway.

"Candace..." Her father's voice went serious, and Candace prepared herself for what was coming next. "I think—"

She cut him off before he had the chance to continue. "No. I don't need a security guard tagging around and smothering me." She shivered just thinking about it. Sure it was sweet that he cared about her well-being, but she simply wanted to live a normal life. "Most people don't know who I am anyway." After the divorce Candace and her mother had both taken on her mother's maiden name for privacy and safety. But of course, there were those few men who, after doing a little digging, had learned her true identity and tried to use her to get to her father.

"Candace, the letters are getting worse. They're far more threatening than they used to be."

She shaded her eyes from the sun and cast a glance around the quaint neighborhood, her focus settling on her two best friends. "Look, Dad, I'm safe here in Connecticut. I'm surrounded by family and friends. And it's probably Ginger herself sending those letters."

A heavy sigh and then, "I miss you, kiddo."

"I miss you too, Dad. Right now I'm swamped with a project but I promise to come see you soon."

"Maybe that's not such a good idea. Not until the police find out who's been sending the letters."

"You don't want me to visit?" she teased, trying to lighten

the mood.

"You know I do, but—"

She let him off the hook and gave a breezy laugh. "It's okay, Dad. I'll be in New York later this fall for the state marathon and we'll get together then." With that they said their goodbyes. Candace slipped her phone back into her pocket and pulled out her iPod.

When she lifted her chin to look at the house, to take one more longing gaze at the stripper before her run, she noticed he was gone. She darted a glance around, but he'd disappeared without a trace. How very stealthy of him. Oh well. Maybe it was for the best. The less temptation the better.

Fully aware of the heat rising inside her lascivious body, Candace tightened her laces before climbing to her feet. She strapped her iPod to her arm and adjusted the buds in her ears before taking off for the running park circling Blueberry Lake—named after its super clean, crystal blue water. As she approached the water, she watched the waves lap gently against the embankment, undulating, rippling and reminding her of two salacious bodies coming together, over and over.

Dear God, her sex-deprived body was definitely showing signs of stress. Sure she had a good imagination, but conjuring up images of naked bodies in motion simply from watching the swell was over the top. Perhaps a trip to Toys4Gals for a few extra accessories was in order. Her thoughts raced back to Mr. Shirtless, and she suspected the only way to tamp down the flames inside her was by taking a dip in the water, now likely frigid from the cool autumn nights.

Marc Collins didn't like the way she was watching him. Well, that wasn't entirely true. He liked it. A little too much. And therein lay the problem. Jason Krane had hired him to watch over his daughter, not for his daughter to watch over him—with interest in her eyes.

Sure he needed to get close to her, but there was a fine line between close, and up close and personal, and he knew better than to cross it.

But did she have to be so damn sexy?

With her tight athletic body, curvy in all the right places, long dark hair pulled back into a ponytail and gorgeous green eyes, she made it hard to remember that he was here on an assignment. And that assignment meant staying alert and aware until investigators found whoever was sending Krane those threatening letters. The last thing he wanted to do was get mixed up with his boss's daughter. No, Krane deserved better from him. After all, Marc owed his career to Krane, having gone from set designer to security specialist after halting a crazed stalker on the movie set. Krane, grateful for Marc's quick thinking and bravery, had taken Marc under his wing, had him trained as a security specialist and hired him as one of his own personal bodyguards. He certainly didn't want to betray his boss or jeopardize his position.

When Candace plunked herself down on the grass and answered her phone, Marc left his post and decided a short run was in order, to clear his head—both of them. Right now Candace was safe and sound, surrounded by her coworkers and friends, and he desperately needed a moment of reprieve from those flirtatious eyes of hers.

The soles of his running shoes tapped a steady beat on the path and helped drone out his thoughts of Candace. As a security specialist, keeping fit, alert and healthy was a necessary part of the job, necessary to keep both him and his clients alive.

Perspiration broke out on his skin as he ran long and hard,

exhausting his muscles and focusing his thoughts. He turned his attention from Candace to Pamina, the willowy woman who'd hired him. How fortunate for him that she'd mistaken him for the paint stripper when he'd walked by the house a few days ago, after he'd finished setting up his hidden surveillance cameras.

A sound behind him gained his attention and he turned in time to see Candace closing the distance between them.

The swinging of her ponytail, the flush on her cheeks, her quick rapid breathing and the sight of her gorgeous breasts bouncing with each thrust had his mind racing and his cock throbbing. Despite knowing better, his thoughts took off on an erotic journey, and there wasn't a damn thing he could do about it.

Marc on his back.

Candace on top of him, his hands on her hips.

Her sweet cunt milking his cock.

Fucking...

Christ, what he'd do to amplify that provocative look of hers, and mimic those arousing up and down movements of her lush breasts while they were engaging in other more pleasant yet equally vigorous activities.

Chapter Two

As Candace closed the gap between them, and the sight of Mr. Shirtless's sculpted back muscles and tight sexy ass came into view, moisture broke out on her skin and she suspected it had little to do with the early-morning sun beating down on her. This scrumptious display of man had her mind wandering, envisioning that toned body climbing over her, his mouth crashing down on hers while those big hands of his used her hips for leverage as he powered his cock into her.

With her mind preoccupied and her knees turning to rubber, it was all she could do to maintain a coherent thought. Totally thrown off her stride as she approached the first turn, Candace faltered. Cripes! Before she could slow her pace and find stability she went flying forward. Arms flailing, looking for something to grip on to, her momentum sent her off the beaten path and onto the grassy embankment fringing the lake. Unfortunately not the fall, or the friction of her body sliding over the leafy blades, could slow her down or stop her from sailing head first into the water.

How. Totally. Frigging. Embarrassing.

She opened her mouth to scream but only managed to gurgle as she plunged to the bottom of the lake. The water rushed over her, seeping into her clothes and sneakers and splashing over the bank as she tried to find her footing.

When her feet finally connected with the sandy bottom, she pushed herself out of the water, praying Mr. Shirtless had missed the action and was halfway around the track by now. But when her lids flew open, her stomach plummeted, her day having just gone from bad to worse.

He stood at the embankment, staring down at her. "Jesus, are you okay?"

When she saw genuine concern in his eyes, something inside her softened, and a burst of foreign emotions took a lazy stroll through her body, catching her off guard. Goodness, no man had ever looked at her like that before, with such worry in his eyes, such warmth and compassion, and she didn't quite know what to make of his careful regard.

Feeling color blossom on her cheeks, Candace wiped her bangs from her face and blinked a big drop of water from her lashes. She shook off the adrenaline rush and nodded. "Yes, I'm fine." At least her body was. She couldn't say the same for her ego.

"What happened?"

Without censoring her words and somewhat rattled by the strange way he made her feel, she blurted out, "It was all your fault."

His head jerked back. "How was it my fault?"

"I didn't expect to see you on the track." Candace pulled the buds from her ears, removed her wet iPod from her arm and tossed them onto the grass. Damn thing was probably ruined.

He cocked his head. "Again, how is that my fault?"

Deciding she'd said too much and completely flustered by the whole incident, she looked at him and took note of his sexy smile. "What?" she asked.

His grin widened. "Nothing. It's nothing."

"If it's nothing, then why are you grinning at me like that?"

He shrugged, and his eyes raced over her clothes. In that instant her nipples hardened, and she wondered if he noticed her arousal through her training jacket. So much for the crystal blue water cooling down her lustful body. She was pretty damned sure she'd just heated the entire lake up a few degrees.

"I don't know. I guess it's because you look like a drowned cat."

"Thanks," she shot back and tried to smooth her hair from her face. "I'm glad I could amuse you with my appalling state."

"Not appalling. Adorable."

"Oh." Inexplicably, something in the way he said "adorable" brought warmth to her face, not to mention one other part of her body.

He thinks I'm adorable.

With the back of his hand, he wiped perspiration from his brow. She took pleasure in the sexy shift of his muscles and the heat in his dark eyes as they raked over her. Fire whipped through her veins and she dropped deeper into the water, a futile attempt to tamp down the flames.

"Here give me your hand. Let me help you."

As he reached for her and she saw those big, strong callused hands of his, she did a quick tally. One, it was his fault she'd faltered in the first place. Two, he did get to see her all wet and aroused. And three, he too looked like he could use a little cooling off.

His palm closed over hers and he gave slight tug. She in turn braced her feet, gave a tug of her own and stepped aside as he came crashing into the water next to her.

A moment later he found his footing and stood. His gaze locked on hers and he wiped the water from his eyes. "What the hell—?"

His voice fell off and she guessed he'd read her desire, taking note of the way she was looking at him with longing in her eyes. Water dripped down his chest and she practically salivated, aching to trail those tiny droplets with the tip of her tongue. The cool water settled just above his waistband, prohibiting her from seeing the wet outline of his cock. She swallowed and resisted the urge to dive under the surface for a glimpse. Jesus, she couldn't believe how lusty her thoughts had turned. A result of no sex for the last few months, she supposed.

She did a brief perusal of the area. All was quiet. Not a runner to be found. When she turned back to him, he ran his tongue over his bottom lip, drinking in the refreshing splashes of Blueberry Lake from his mouth. Her gaze centered on his luscious lips and her libido roared for attention, demanding she do something about her sex life or lack thereof.

Maybe one little kiss, one quick romp in the water would help clear her head. Heck, it wasn't in her nature to just jump into bed with a man—a stranger, at that—and she could hardly believe the direction her brain had gone. After all, she didn't even know his name. Then again, maybe that was a good thing. He was nearly finished with the job at the inn and come nightfall she'd never set eyes on him again. Tomorrow she'd be refreshed and ready to go back to celibate Candace, no one the wiser that she'd gotten a little sidetracked.

He must have read her mind. His eyes darkened and turned serious. She watched his throat work as he swallowed, and he moved a measured step closer. As his body loomed over hers, he dipped his head and for a brief moment she thought he was going to kiss her. He reached out and pushed her hair off her face. She tipped her head to meet his gaze, and when a low moan rose up from her throat, something flashed in his eyes and he hesitated. A second later he gave his head a brisk shake, as if to clear it. Then he took a distancing step back and walked to the embankment.

What the heck?

"So we're even then?" Even though he'd tried for light, she could hear the underlying lust in his voice.

"Even? Why would we be even?"

"You said it was my fault you fell into the lake. I can only assume that's why you pulled me in here with you. To square things up? A little tit for tat?" When she didn't respond, he turned to her. "Wasn't that your reason, Candace?"

"Yeah, that was my reason." One of many, but he didn't need to know that just yet. Then something else occurred to her and she tightened, memories of the threatening letters filling her thoughts. Suddenly feeling very foolish and very vulnerable, she questioned, "How do you know my name?"

Without missing a beat he said, "I heard your friends call out to you. Earlier, at the inn."

"Oh, right." She'd forgotten he was within earshot when Lindsay and Anna had greeted her as she stretched on the front lawn.

"I'm Marc. Marc Collins." He held his hand out, and as she shook it, she studied him a moment. Good guys were rare, but something in her gut told her Marc Collins just might be one of them, not that she'd always been such a great judge of character. But he had a strength of character about him, unlike the men she usually found herself attracted to. It also occurred to her that he gave off a protective vibe, making her feel absurdly safe with him. Truthfully, there was something about this man. Something trustworthy and fiercely protective that put her at ease.

Intuition told her she had nothing to fear from him. That he

107

was a gentleman, a man of integrity. She considered things a minute longer. Marc was a paint stripper hired by Pamina, not some aspiring actor using her to get close to her father—heck he didn't even respond to her advances, which proved he was different from any other man she'd ever met. And the painstaking care he took with his work proved he was a skilled laborer.

Candace was pretty damn certain he didn't know who she was. Was there a chance there could be something more between them, that he could like her for who she really was, not for her daddy's power and influence? Damned if she didn't want to find out. But sadly, he hadn't tried to hit on her. Even when presented with the opportunity.

That was definitely something she'd have to rectify.

Marc mentally gave himself a good hard scolding and lectured himself on keeping his hands off her, despite the sexual sparks arcing between them. What the hell had he been thinking? He'd nearly kissed her. Thank God common sense had dictated, and sound reason found its way back into his brain before he did something he'd regret later. Yeah, later. Because he certainly wouldn't regret it while he was doing it with her. Oh no. Not at all. If he had her in his arms, he'd enjoy every damn minute of it. Exploring that curvaceous body of hers, kissing that lush mouth, running his thumbs and his tongue over her gorgeous pink nipples. Yeah, he'd glimpsed those pert buds through her track jacket. All hard and swollen and begging for his mouth.

His cock swelled almost painfully, and he shifted to hide his arousal. Marc clenched his jaw to stifle a moan and moved to the embankment. He turned to her. "Need a hand?"

Her eyes snapped up, as if she too had been lost in

thought. "No, I'm good, thanks."

She climbed from the water and he followed behind her. She grabbed her iPod, murmured something under her breath about it being ruined, and walked to the running track. When she reached the trail, she turned to him, soaking wet. A cool fall breeze blew over them and she gave a slight shiver. As he took in the bedraggled sight of her, his protective instincts kicked into high gear. Sure he was a security specialist, a bodyguard for a living, but whatever had suddenly come over him went deeper than that. Candace was strong and capable, but there was a guarded vulnerability in her eyes that really got to him. Had she been hurt in the past?

She jerked her thumb toward the inn. "I need to head back."

"I'm with you on that."

Candace scanned the length of him, then her eyes widened, almost apologetically. "I never thought. You probably don't have a change of clothes with you."

"I do. In my van. I come equipped." He neglected to tell her that his van also came equipped with a security camera, recording their actions even now, as they stood there staring at each other.

She exhaled a relieved breath and began to make her way back. "Good. I'd hate to cost you a day's work by having you go home to change."

Jesus, how refreshing. Marc was used to hanging around pampered movie stars who didn't give a rat's ass if their actions resulted in him losing a day's work. Candace really was different from those divas. She seemed so natural, so down to earth.

Marc hurried his steps to catch up and decided to probe for information. If he was going to protect her without her knowledge, he needed to know more about her.

"How long have you been a designer?"

"Officially for about five years now. Although, in reality more like twenty-five."

"Twenty-five?"

She laughed. "Yeah, Lindsay, Anna and I have been tearing our rooms apart and putting them back together since we were kids."

Testing her, he said, "Your mom and dad must have loved that."

She hesitated for a moment before continuing, "Oh, they sure did. I can't tell you how many times they grounded me until I put everything in order again."

The fact that she included her father in the picture didn't elude him. "Tell me, Candace, what do you do for fun in Mason Creek?"

"You mean you're not from around here?"

Damn. So much for blending in as a local and keeping his cover. It was a small town, yet still big enough that not everyone knew everyone else. "I'm new in town. Been sleeping in my van until my new shop is ready." He resisted the urge to cringe at his bold-faced lie.

"New shop?"

"Yeah, new workshop," he said, not bothering to elaborate.

"Your parents aren't from around here?"

"No. We're from the city." He neglected to tell her which city.

"Relatives?"

"No."

"Then what brings a city boy to Mason Creek?"

He gestured toward his van. "Work. So you never did tell me what you do around here for fun."

Ignoring his comment, she said, "Maybe once we get the inn finished, you'll be able to get a room until your place is ready." She crinkled her nose and her green eyes glistened in the sunlight. "On the other hand, maybe it's not such a great idea."

"Why?"

"Well, I never thought to consider—"

"Consider what?"

"That any of the rooms would appeal to you."

He furrowed his brow, confused. "Why wouldn't they appeal to me?"

"It's just that, well, we're designing fantasy-inspired theme rooms."

That took him by surprise. "Really?"

Candace grinned. "Yeah, really."

"You mean to tell me Pamina hired you to create sex rooms?"

She nodded and chuckled lightly, obviously enjoying the easy flow of conversation as much as he was. "I know. Who would have thought? She doesn't seem the type, does she?"

Suddenly intrigued, he said, "Speaking of types, tell me more about these rooms and exactly what you're planning on doing with yours."

Chapter Three

Oh God, she was smitten.

As they walked back to the inn, she described with both enthusiasm and detail how she wanted to create a room designed for stamina to accommodate the actively inclined. With genuine interest, Marc listened to her ramble on, and she really liked that about him. Most men couldn't care less about what she had to say and would tune her out whenever she talked about her work. But not Marc. He really paid attention to every detail, even asking intelligent questions, making her wonder if he had a background in design.

She enjoyed talking to him, and it occurred to her that they had a lot in common, a lot of similar interests. Candace appreciated the way his dark passionate eyes widened with intrigue and fascination as she described her concepts, and the way that nice mouth of his turned up at the corners when he smiled or probed for more information. He was strong and protective and so damn adorable, it had her feeling all weird inside. Just being in his presence, standing close to that hewn body of his, had her all worked up.

They reached the house and Marc glanced at her clothes. "I guess you'd better get changed."

She perused his now-dry chest, and as her fingers tingled with longing to touch him, she resisted the urge to run her hands along his body.

"You too." Except neither made a move to go. They both stood there, enjoying the conversation and the easy intimacy blossoming between them.

Just then Pamina stepped outside and made her way toward them, her long, lithe body practically floating over the walkway. She called out to Candace as she approached.

Candace grabbed her ponytail to wring it out. As water slid down her chest, Marc cleared his throat and took a step back. "It looks like you're needed, and you'd better get changed. You're dripping."

Oh, he had no idea.

Candace nodded and could barely pull her focus away as he made his way to his van. Pamina touched her on the arm. "I see you've met Marc."

Before Candace could respond, Pamina's fat cat Abra jumped into Candace's arms and licked a water droplet off her chest.

"Whoa," Candace said as his wet scratchy tongue pulled her thoughts back.

"Abra," Pamina admonished and tapped him on the nose, a gentle reproach. "You keep that up and you'll never convince me you've changed your ways."

As Candace watched the exchange, she grinned. What a strange relationship this mystical woman had with her cat. Sometimes she treated him like he was human. Then again, maybe he was. Perhaps Pamina really was a magical being and had turned him into a feline as punishment for misconduct. He did seem to be quite the devilish little feline. When Abra gave a loud purr, Candace scoffed at her crazy imagination, pushed those ridiculous thoughts aside and focused on the task ahead.

"Pamina," she began as Abra jumped from her arms and leisurely made his way to Marc's van. "I think I'm going to have to hire a carpenter to help out with the room. I need some sturdy furniture made. Sturdier than I can purchase."

Pamina's long golden hair blew in the early-morning breeze and she narrowed her knowledgeable eyes in thought. "Do you have a carpenter in mind?"

"I usually use a local guy—"

"I'll do it."

Candace didn't have to turn around to know who'd spoken. There was only one man who had such a deep sexy voice. Lust shot through her body at his rich desirous tone. She took a brief moment to gather herself before she spun to face him and tried for normal.

"You can build furniture?" He'd changed into a worn pair of jeans that hugged his body in all the right places, and a white T-shirt did wonders for his upper torso. Scrumptious.

"Yes, I'm good with my hands." His grin was slow and he fixed her with a look that told her just how capable he was. She sucked in a breath and a fine shiver moved through her as heat arched between them. God, she wanted him. Oh how she wanted him. Masking her enthusiasm, she clamped her thighs and pretended to ponder his offer for a moment.

"What a great idea, Marc," Pamina said. "For your services, we can offer you room and board as well."

Marc gave her an odd look. "How do you know—?"

Without answering his question, Pamina continued. "It's just me and Abra in this big old place and we quite enjoy the company. Like the girls, you're welcome to the pantry and all the facilities, including the shower. I understand that such an undertaking can sometimes get a little messy." Then she turned to Candace. "What do you think?"

114

I think things are going to get a whole lot more interesting.

She cast Marc a glance and examined his sensual mouth, wondering how it would feel on her body, and deciding then and there that she most definitely needed to find out. Now how to get him to make a move on her?

"Sometimes I work late."

He pushed his hands into his jeans, pulling them low on his hips. "I don't mind working late."

"If you're rooming here, I might keep you up."

In more ways than one.

"I don't mind being kept up."

Visions of him being...*up*...while the two of them were working out the kinks in her fantasy room raced through her mind. She swallowed down a moan and held her hand out.

"Welcome aboard."

Just off the back deck, Marc leaned over the table saw and ran a piece of wood through the sharp blade. He'd forgotten how much he liked working with his hands and building things. He glanced around, taking note of the birds chirping and the simple life outside the city. This was definitely something he could get used to.

He turned his attention back to constructing the sturdy king-sized bed Candace had designed, a bed created for marathon sex. As he worked, he tried to convince himself that he'd volunteered for the job so he could keep a better eye on Candace. Not because he wanted to be in that bedroom with her. Up close and personal.

He'd been working with her for a couple of days now, helping her carry in sex equipment, which included a Tantra chair, a sex swing, some strange-looking glider, and a dance pole that, he had to admit, was a personal favorite. He also had to admit it was becoming harder and harder to keep his hands off her lush body, especially with the way she continually looked at him, lust smoldering in the depths of her passionate green eyes. And Christ, when he'd helped her secure the floor-to-ceiling pole and watched her swing around it to ensure it was safe and bolted correctly, it was all he could do not to imagine her shimmying down it—naked. Her teasing and taunting had him walking around with a constant boner. If she was waiting for him to make the first move, she could forget it. No way, no how was he going to seduce her.

He *had* to keep his hands to himself, as much as that seemed to frustrate her. And him. He owed it to Krane. If this assignment proved successful, all his hard work over the last year was going to pay off and Krane was going to offer him the job as head of security, moving him up the ladder a few rungs.

He pulled the board away, made his way to the side of the house for another piece of lumber, and spotted Candace and Anna walking down the driveway. A quick glance at his watch told him it was lunchtime and he wondered why Lindsay wasn't joining them for a bite to eat. Come to think of it, he hadn't seen Lindsay in a few days. In passing, he had come across the carpenter she'd hired to help her tear down a wall, and with the way he looked at Lindsay, Marc wondered if he too was having a hell of a time focusing on the job. Then again there was always the masonry guy, who'd been keeping an awfully close eye on Anna.

He didn't miss the sexy look Candace cast his way as she sauntered down the sidewalk. His cock thickened when she gave a sexy shake of her ass. What the hell was the little spitfire trying to do to him anyway? Didn't she know he was working with power tools?

And one tool in particular was swelling at an alarming rate.

Fuck...

He dropped the boards and peeled off his shirt as he made his way to his van, knowing he had to follow close behind. Close enough to keep her in sight but far enough to remain inconspicuous. Perhaps a run would help him let off some steam. Before he reached the door, Pamina suddenly appeared before him, coming out of nowhere. Maybe he'd been so lost in his thoughts he hadn't heard her approach.

"She's a lovely girl, don't you think?" Insightful eyes met his, and for a brief moment he wondered if she knew how lusty his thoughts had been for the last few days.

"Yeah, lovely," he responded.

Pamina smoothed her golden hair from her face and gestured toward his pile of lumber. "She was lucky to have found someone who could build furniture on such short notice."

He gave an easy shrug. "I guess I was at the right place at the right time."

She pursed her lips and studied him for a long moment before saying, "Funny about that, isn't it?"

Suddenly uncomfortable, Marc shifted. Christ, did she know who he was?

"She's not one to just hire someone on the spot."

"No?" Marc looked past her shoulders and glimpsed Candace before she disappeared around the corner with her friend.

"No, she's careful who she associates with." Pamina leaned in close and lowered her voice in secrecy. "You see her daddy is a big New York director. In the past men have tried to get close to her, wining and dining and deceiving her in order to get in with her father. Which is why she's sworn off men, I suppose."

117

"She's sworn off men?" That must have been the guarded vulnerable look he'd spotted in her eyes. Men had been using her—betraying her. Catching him off guard, anger raced through him, and he wanted to find and pummel every guy who had hurt her. His jaw clenched and his nostrils flared, and he wondered when protecting her had become so personal to him.

"Yes, so she must really trust you if she hired you without doing a background check. You must have made a very big impression on her."

He swallowed, guilt closing in on him from all angles. He wasn't using her, but he *was* deceiving her because he'd been pretending to be a handyman. He had strict orders to keep his identity a secret.

"I see," he said, for lack of anything better.

Pamina put her hand on his shoulder. "But you and I both know you'd never deceive her, isn't that right?"

"Yeah, that's right," he agreed and sidestepped her, knowing he had to get going before Candace was too far out of his sight. "If you'll excuse me. I'm late for my run."

Marc slipped into a T-shirt and his running shorts, and jogged down the sidewalk. He took the corner he'd seen Candace negotiate earlier. As he made his way along the main street, he spotted the two women having lunch inside a quaint curbside café. He continued to run, keeping the door to the café within sight at all times. A short while later Candace and Anna exited the building and walked back to the inn. Maintaining a reasonable pace behind them, Marc kept her under surveillance. Once she stepped inside the inn, safe and sound, surrounded by her friends, he decided to take a quick jaunt around Blueberry Lake to give his muscles a good, strenuous workout.

As he approached the spot where Candace had pulled him

into the water, his pace slowed and his mind raced, recalling the way her nipples had tightened beneath her tracksuit. He spent a long moment staring at the water and considered taking a dip to cool himself down.

"Going in?"

He tightened at the sound of her voice behind him. When he spun around and took in the warm flush on her cheeks, the sexy way her nipples pressed against her tank top and the way her long, tanned legs looked in her provocative short shorts, he almost gave in to temptation.

The hungry look in her eyes made him ache. Fuck he wanted her so badly, he could barely think straight. Pleasure raced through him, and his cock swelled inside his running shorts. Candace cast a glance down, and when her eyes traveled back to his face, they were gleaming with mischief. Okay, he needed to put a stop to this and he needed to do it now.

As he ran over every reason to back away, he said, "Candace, I—"

Jesus, what was he going to tell her? That he was hired by her father to watch over her? That he wasn't who she thought he was? The last thing he wanted to do was hurt her or deceive her. After all, she trusted him enough to try to seduce him.

Okay, he needed to put some distance between them. But when she went up on her tippy toes and put her mouth close to his, every reason he had for keeping his distance suddenly dissolved.

"I think going for a swim is a great idea." The soft seduction in her voice pulled him in and shattered any semblance of control he thought he had.

Without warning, she climbed into the water. At the sight of her gorgeous, wet body, need exploded inside him.

Ah, Jesus...

Unable to contain the heat rising in him, he jumped into the water with her, knowing there was only one way to feed the hunger gnawing at his insides. When she stepped close, and skin touched skin, she poised her mouth open in invitation. His cock took over where his brain left off and his lips crashed down on hers. Aware of her desire, he gripped her by the hips and pulled her to him, meshing their bodies together and lining up their nether regions. When he pushed his cock against her pussy, she gyrated and moaned into his mouth.

As the warm afternoon sun beat down on them, it occurred to him that they were outdoors, in plain sight. Hell, he needed to get behind closed doors with her before someone stumbled upon them. "The path...people." He felt a tremor move through her and realized how much that excited her. He gave a low, heated laugh, intrigued by her boldness. "I had no idea you were so naughty," he whispered into her mouth.

Her laughter churned with passion and expressive eyes brimmed with desire. "Neither did I. Until just now. You must bring that out in me." She cupped his cock and gave a gentle squeeze. "Now let's see what I can bring out in you."

Christ, he knew better than to get intimate with her—especially in public—but the look in her eyes and the thrill it gave her to play this little exhibitionist game prompted him into action. Every damn reason he had for staying away from her suddenly seemed so insignificant, and giving her everything she ever wanted had become more important than his own well-being.

He gripped her tank top and peeled it over her head, exposing her luscious breasts. With pleasure racing through him, Marc moaned and wet his mouth. "So beautiful," he murmured and brushed the pad of his thumb over one perfect nipple.

She arched into him, and he could hear the note of desperation lacing her voice when she asked, "Would you like a taste?"

Cravings like he'd never before experienced swamped him. "Hell, you know I would." Trembling and entirely lost in the moment, he inclined his head and drew her hard bud into his mouth. *Fuck...* Her fingers raked through his hair and held him tight. As she swelled in his mouth, she gave a low erotic whimper and he damn near erupted on the spot.

Her hands raced over him with aroused eagerness, tugging at his shirt and shorts almost frantically. Wanting to slow her down so they could enjoy and savor every sinful moment, he inched back, gripped her hands and placed them at her sides. His gaze moved to hers, and when his glance was met with heat, passion and vulnerability swirling around in a sea of green, his heart softened and everything inside him reached out to her. Tenderness stole over him as emotions gathered in a knot deep in his gut, and he instinctively knew he had to make this good for her. So damn good it would help her fight every last demon that plagued her darkest corner.

He pitched his voice low. "Come here, sweetheart."

She stepped into him and he backed her up against the embankment. Once he had her caged between his body and the grass, he leaned in for a slow soul-searching kiss.

She tugged at him, heat reflecting in her eyes. "Easy, baby," he responded, and once again secured her hands to her sides.

Their gazes collided. "Marc, please..."

Reining in his lust, he took in the erotic sight of her and the way she had so readily opened up to him, trusting him with her pleasure. "You can beg all you want," he assured her with a grin, as the cool water lapped at his waist. "But I'm not in any hurry. Now that I have you where I want you, I'm going to leisurely explore your body." With that he gently shaped her contours, kneading her flesh and enjoying the feel of her soft curves in his palms. His mouth moved to her neck. With slow, easy movements, he properly introduced himself to her. Trailing lower, he paid homage to her breasts using his hands, mouth and tongue, sucking, nibbling and licking and taking his sweet-ass time before moving to her belly button, which was just inches out of the water.

Needing to go lower, he lifted her by the hips and set her on the bank, lining her pussy up with his mouth. He gripped her shorts and toyed with the waistband.

"Marc...?"

"Yeah, babe." The strange look on her face spoke volumes. She didn't understand his slow seduction, his need to please her. Didn't understand that it gave him pleasure just to pleasure her.

Her eyes clouded and he felt a curious shift inside him. "I...I—"

"I know, babe. Really, I do." And he did know. That every asshole she'd been with had cared more about his needs than hers. Deciding to show her another side of lovemaking, Marc proceeded to inch her shorts down her silky legs, leaving her lacy panties behind.

She sat before him, quivering, her eyes watching his every move carefully. She reached for him, to touch him in return, her soft hands greedily sliding over his skin, and even though he liked it, he anchored her hands to her sides, intent on making this all about her.

Candace inched her legs open and when the enticing scent of her arousal hit him, he damn near lost all his hard-fought control. As desire slammed into him, he drew a deep, labored breath and tried to tame his raging erection as it begged him to answer the pull in his groin.

Turning his focus back to Candace, he touched the lace of her panties, running the fabric through his fingers as he leaned forward and licked her sweet pussy through the thin material.

She gave a low moan of longing that nearly drove him to his knees. Steadying himself between her legs, he darted a quick glance upward and watched the way her eyes glazed with desire. The heat on her cheeks and the way she looked at him with such lust, such want, filled him with an unfamiliar need. Jesus, he loved that he'd put that look on her face and he couldn't deny that bringing pleasure to her, taking painstaking care of her every craving, made him feel all weird inside.

"Widen your legs for me." As emotions and sensations ripped through him, he hardly recognized his own voice. He drew a breath to center himself and questioned what it was about her that softened his resolve and made him feel fiercely protective.

He gripped her thighs as she widened them, granting him access to her most private places. Using the tip of his index finger, he pushed the lace to the side to expose her pubis. With slow, deliberate movements, he stroked her groomed strip of silky wet dark hair, his thumb purposely brushing over her engorged clit. Undeniably, she had the nicest pussy he'd ever set eyes on.

"Mmm, nice." As he continued to stroke her, he leaned in for a taste. Her hips came off the bank as he lightly brushed his tongue over her cunt.

"Oh God, Marc," she cried out, and he wondered if anyone in the vicinity had heard her. But none of that mattered right now. All that mattered was getting his fill of her pussy and making her come for him.

As he indulged in her heat, she grew wetter and her sweet cream tasted like candy as it dripped languidly down his chin. He could tell she was close by the way her body was quivering, but he wasn't quite ready to bring her over the precipice. He slipped a finger inside her and stilled.

Fuck... She was so goddamn tight that his cock ached to replace his digit. He was ready to erupt just from the feel of her firm walls closing around him.

Panting, she gyrated, letting him know in no uncertain terms what she wanted. As his finger slipped in deeper, he circled her clit with his tongue. He gave a light caress over the bundle of nerves inside her pussy and when she cried out, he nearly went out of his mind. Need exploded inside him and his balls ached so badly it was all he could do to breathe.

He gave another brush over her G-spot and watched her eyes flare hot. "You like that do you?" he managed to get out.

Instead of answering, she slipped her hands around his head and guided his mouth back to her pussy, which was wet and glistening under the afternoon sun. Chuckling at her boldness, he slipped another finger inside, and she arched into him. As he moved his finger in and out, finding a nice steady rhythm, he licked her engorged clit and rolled it between his teeth. The dual assault quickly pushed her over the edge and in no time at all breath rushed from her lungs and her feminine scent filled the air.

"Marc," she cried out, as she reached the edge of oblivion.

"That's it, Candace. Let me taste you."

Her sweet nectar poured into his mouth and he let loose a groan of pleasure, his body needy for her in ways that left him speechless.

He worked his tongue over her cunt, drinking in every last drop and soothing her swollen sex with the soft pad of his thumb. After her muscles stopped spasming, he inched back to look at her naked body, and she slipped into the water with him.

With a new air of contentment about her, she laced her hands around his neck and pulled his mouth to hers. She kissed him. Deeply. Her tongue sliding inside his mouth in the most seductive manner. Jesus, she was a damn good kisser. She moved to his neck and her long lashes fluttered against his skin, eliciting a shudder from deep within. Her hand slipped between their bodies and she palmed his massive erection. Marc moaned and pressed against her.

The sound of running shoes slapped against the ground and pulled his attention away. "Candace—"

"Mmm," she murmured as her hand inched inside his shorts.

He was so damn hard, he could barely keep a coherent thought. He pressed his body over hers, shielding her from the joggers, and spoke in whispered words.

"Someone's coming."

She gave him an odd look, then he got a clue. "Not me," he assured her, then gestured with a nod. "Joggers."

Her eyes widened in understanding. "Oh."

"We need to go."

Confusion clouded her eyes. "But what about you? I haven't—"

He pressed his finger to her lips. "I wanted this to be about you, Candace." Her mouth slowly inched open and she blinked, not at all understanding what he was getting at.

"What about your pleasure?"

"What you don't understand, babe, is I'm happy just to satisfy you."

She stood there staring at him for a long moment, then as comprehension dawned, she touched his face. When their eyes met and locked, warmth blanketed them and a strange new intimacy pulled him under.

"Who are you?" she asked, her voice teasing. "And when did you land on Earth?"

They shared a laugh and with their bodies melded together, she ran her finger over his cheek, then traced the outline of his mouth, her eyes moving over his face, her gaze caressing, probing. His muscles rippled and his breathing grew shallow as her gentle touch went right through him. Heat bombarded him and all he could think about was ripping off his clothes and ramming his cock all the way up inside her.

He gathered himself and transferred his thoughts back to the present, realizing exactly who he was. The man who was hired to watch over her, not fuck her.

Bloody hell.

Chapter Four

With her legs rubbery and a permanent smile etched on her flushed face, Candace made her way back to the inn, Marc at her side. A comfortable silence fell over them as birds chirped and nestled in the huge apple trees beside the house. Juicy red apples weighed down the branches and glistened beneath the sun. Candace did a double take. She had a designer's eye that took in everything, but she certainly couldn't remember ever seeing those ripe trees before.

When she reached the front lawn she turned to Marc, and the heated look in his eyes had her aching to go back to the lake, to touch and kiss him all over, the way he'd touched and kissed her. Her mouth watered and liquid heat poured through her veins in anticipation.

He nodded toward the power tools. "I'd better get back to work."

"Me too," she said, not really interested in moving anywhere without him but knowing she needed to get the painting completed before Marc finished the bed and brought it inside. They also had to work together to install the hanging sex swing, position the love glider and Tantra chair. All devices that combined sex and exercise. Not to mention the already installed floor-to-ceiling pole, which was perfect for dancing, an excellent cardiovascular workout.

Marc leaned close and for a second she thought he was going to kiss her, then once again she saw something in his eyes before he stepped back, abruptly. Hesitation. One minute he was making crazy love to her with his hands and mouth, and the next he was pulling back, physically and emotionally. The same way he had earlier, during their first trip into the water.

A loud noise inside the house drew their attention, and Candace jumped. Marc laughed and his knuckles brushed her skin, a comforting gesture. "There seems to be quite a bit of banging going on up there."

She wouldn't mind doing a little banging of her own. "Must be Brad tearing down that wall."

Marc inclined his head, and heat churned in his eyes. "Yeah, must be," he agreed, his voice deeper, huskier. When she caught the strange look moving over his face, she followed his gaze. For a brief second she thought she caught the outline of Lindsay pressed against the window, but the image disappeared as quickly as it had appeared.

Marc cleared his throat, suddenly flustered, and she wondered exactly what he'd seen in that window. What was going on up there?

"You'd better get back at it," he said. "I'm close to finishing the bedframe."

With that they both went back to the task at hand. Candace made her way through the old house, calling out to Pamina but unable to find her anywhere. Everyone was hard at work, she supposed. She hurried up the gorgeous winding staircase, climbed into her coveralls and readied her supplies.

Now here she was, her mind wandering, thinking about how she wanted to set up the furniture and how she'd like to try out every sinful piece with Marc. God, she couldn't believe how intimate she'd been with him, a man she barely knew but felt completely comfortable with. A man who was concerned with her needs and desires, and admitted that pleasuring her had pleasured him. Nor could she believe how he'd so easily read her, and the excitement she felt from having sex outdoors with the possibility of getting caught. A fine shiver moved down her spine and she knew she wanted to do that again.

He had to be some visiting alien, she decided.

But seriously, who was he and where had he come from? He'd only recently moved to Mason Creek. Where had he moved from, and where exactly was this shop he was setting up? Perhaps Pamina would know, since she'd hired him in the first place.

And why did he go from hot to cold so quickly, displaying passion one second and hesitation the next?

As she pondered that longer, wondering if past hurts were holding him back, Candace wiped her brow, then put the finishing touches on the back wall. She stood back to admire her work. Satisfied with the job and happy she was half-done with only two walls left, she glanced out the window and spotted Marc walking to his van. Would he be sleeping in there tonight? She noted the king-sized mattress on her floor, brand-new sheets and plush comforter beside it. Sure the room wasn't ready yet, but even if he didn't get the frame made, there was no reason why he couldn't crash on that perfectly comfortable makeshift bed.

Returning to matters, Candace went to work on finishing her painting just as Abra came sauntering into the room.

"Hey, kitty." She stopped to give him a pat.

Abra curled around her legs, brushing up against her and purring in delight. She stroked his massive underbelly and made a tsking sound.

"You know, Abra, maybe you should come on one of my

runs. It wouldn't hurt you to shed a few pounds."

With that he hissed and hopped up onto her windowsill, where he gave her his back and proceeded to groom himself.

Candace laughed at his ornery behavior. "You really are a strange kitty." Paying him no more attention, she went back to painting. Day bled into night as Candace completed the walls and cleaned up her supplies. The grumbling of her stomach told her it was dinnertime.

When she heard loud banging noises coming from Lindsay's room, she thought about investigating, but Anna popped her head in, her cheeks flushed, her big blue eyes wide and glossy.

"You okay?" Candace asked and furrowed her brow in concern.

"Fine, just wanted to let you know I can't meet up for dinner after all. Looks like we'll be working well into the night."

Candace frowned. Lindsay had been unable to join them for lunch and she could only assume she was still too busy to quit for the night. "Is your project going okay? Do you need help?"

"No," Anna rushed out. "We're right on schedule. But my masonry guy doesn't want to leave smack-dab in the middle of the…job."

Okay, so why did she pause before saying *job*? What exactly was going on in there anyway? Not that it was any of Candace's business. After all, she'd broken the pact. Or had she? Did oral sex count as breaking the pact? Nah, she didn't think so. She'd simply dented it. Only full-blown intercourse counted as breaking it, right?

And if she'd gone so far as to dent it…

"Will you be driving home tonight?" Anna asked.

"Yeah, why? Do you want me to wait and give you a lift?"

"No, I just wouldn't want to keep you up with any noise next door. Laying brick can get noisy."

"No worries, I'm heading home."

"I'll see you in the morning," she said, a twinkle in her eye as she disappeared. Feeling fatigued, Candace carried her brushes to the washtub on the main level, off the laundry area, and rinsed them out. Once her task was complete, she pulled off her coveralls, hopped into a warm shower and washed herself up before heading back to the room to climb into a fresh pair of clothes, which she always brought with her when there was a possibility of staying overnight on a job. She moved through the old inn in search of Pamina but when she couldn't find her, she stepped out into the night.

A refreshing burst of cool evening air brushed over her, giving her a second wind, and her eyes went from Marc's van to the track and back to his van again. There was nothing she liked better than a brisk run after sunset, then maybe she'd grab something to eat.

She wondered if Marc was interested in eating with her...

Marc paced in his van with half of his brain kicking his ass for his stupidity at the lake and the other half unable to stop thinking about the way Candace had felt in his arms or tasted on his tongue. Wincing, he dropped to his small desk chair and ran his hands through his hair, noting that the erotic scent of her still lingered on his skin. Jesus...

Restless in his wobbly seat, he moved from side to side and turned on his security monitors. Apprehension moved through him as he zeroed in on the camera overlooking the lake. Son of a bitch! He'd been so caught up in the moment he'd forgotten the camera had been on them, recording their every salacious action. He held his hand over the delete button, knowing he had to remove any evidence of them together, but then suddenly, he couldn't seem to bring himself to do it just yet. Perhaps a quick look, purely for research purposes, he assured himself, to confirm that the cameras were in working order before he deleted the entire file. He hit the rewind button, taking it back to the exact time he'd jumped into the water.

The erotic sight of him pleasuring Candace came on screen and he immediately hardened. His cock thickened and his balls tightened, demanding he finally do something about his rock-hard erection before he went off like a supernova.

Groaning and feeling like a hormonal teenager, he slipped his hands inside his shorts, gripped his cock and began to stroke himself. Hard. If he wanted to get his mind back on the job, the only way to do it was with a clear head. Both of them. And if this was the answer, then so be it.

When he heard Candace's cries of ecstasy, he pumped faster, the need to release the brewing pressure inside him growing at an alarming rate. Another low groan crawled out of his throat as he worked his palm over his throbbing cock. He closed his eyes briefly, letting his wild imagination take him back to that lake with Candace.

Erotic visions of the way she'd offered herself to him filled his thoughts; her pussy poised at his mouth and his fingers pumping inside her and brushing over her G-spot until she quaked with urgency. Jesus he loved how he'd made her quake.

He opened his eyes in time to watch the way he licked her pussy, his face moving between her thighs and inching open her swollen lips as he ravished her sweet spot. With his senses exploding he dragged in air and knew his orgasm was only a stroke away. His hands began to work harder over his dick as he fantasized how it would feel to slide his cock into her tight sex, and pump in and out of her until they both shattered into a million pieces, their orgasms overtaking them and leaving them drained, sated.

"Fuck..." He moaned out loud as pressure mounted inside him. He cupped his sac and stroked his dick faster. With his cock thickening to the point of no return, he bit down on his bottom lip, his brain no longer functioning.

But then, seconds before he found release, a knock came on his door and had his mind careening back. He grunted something incoherent, summoned what little brainpower he had left and flicked off the monitors, praying that whoever was on the other side of that door hadn't heard anything.

The knock came again, and he worked to stuff his swollen cock back into his shorts and adjust his T-shirt to hide the huge bulge.

"Marc, are you in there?"

Holy hell!

He cleared his throat. "Yeah, just a second," he bit out and drew on an old teenage trick, thinking about sports and old television shows, in an effort to shrink his erection.

"Is everything okay?"

Hell no, everything wasn't okay. Here he was whacking off in a van while he watched himself pleasure his boss's daughter on video. Not only that. He liked her. Really liked her. Candace was open, giving, fun and refreshing. She was natural and lacked pretense. So unlike any other woman he'd ever met. And what was he doing in return? Deceiving her.

"Yeah, I'll be right out." After taming his arousal, he erased the video, drew a centering breath and pulled open the door. He stepped out and inched the door closed behind him, but the minute she leaned forward, breaching his personal space, a rush of sexual energy hit him. Hard.

"What was that noise I heard?"

Feeling flustered, something that never happened to him—until he set eyes on Candace, that is—he rushed out. "Radio...yeah, the radio."

She tried to look past his shoulders, but he moved, blocking her path and slamming his door tight.

"Are you finished for the day?" she asked.

"All done." He put his hands into the pockets of his shorts to inconspicuously adjust himself. Christ, everything about her reduced him to a hormonal juvenile.

"I was just thinking about taking a run, then afterwards grabbing something to...*eat*."

Marc's heart missed a beat as he took in the lust in her eyes and something about the way she said *eat* had his libido roaring to life once again. He should say no and just get the hell out of there and ask his boss to put someone else on the case. But he didn't trust anyone else to look out for her. *Or touch her.*

That last thought made him realize he'd gotten himself in deep.

Too deep.

If he knew what was good for him, he'd just get the fuck out of Dodge. Tonight.

She began to back up, picking up the pace to give herself a head start. "Come on. I'll race you to the lake. Winner takes all," she said with a mischievous gleam in her eyes. When she turned her back to him and took off on a flat-out run, he bent down and tightened his laces.

So it would appear he *didn't* know what was good for him, after all.

Chapter Five

Candace darted a glance over her shoulder to see if he was coming as she raced to the lake. Oh yeah, he was coming all right, and quickly closing the distance between them. A smile pulled at her and she knew if she wanted to win this race she'd better put everything she had into it. Deciding to do just that, Candace lengthened her stride, but Marc was too fast and too strong.

He caught up to her in seconds flat and hadn't broken a sweat yet. "What exactly do you mean, winner takes all?" he asked, keeping pace beside her.

"You see," she managed through labored breathing, knowing she needed to throw him off his stride the same way he'd thrown her off her game the other day. She planned to win the race using any means possible. "*When* I win, I'm going to take you back to the inn and show you another way to exercise."

His eyes lit. "Yeah, how?" She could see the genuine interest in his gaze.

"Well there is the new Tantra chair I'd like to try out. You know, to ensure it works properly and is sturdy enough before we open the room to guests." She watched his face change as understanding dawned. Deciding to play, to push him a little more, she added, "And then there's the hanging sex swing, the love glider and the floor-to-ceiling pole for a little seductive dancing."

His jaw dropped and his stride slowed, his body language conveying his shock at her boldness. Or perhaps he was too busy thinking about what they could do on said equipment to focus on running. Fortunately his reprieve gave her the opportunity she needed to win. Once she reached the embankment, she stopped running and twisted around to glimpse Marc, who still stood there gawking at her, need and desire flitting across his handsome face.

He quickly caught up to her, grabbed her hips and anchored her to him, and her entire body shivered in sensual delight. He put his back to a tree and cast a glance around. "What the hell are you trying to do to me?"

There was something about the way he moved, talked and continually scanned the area that reminded her of a cop or a bodyguard. With her father's line of work, she'd been around enough of them to pick up on their little nuances.

But as heat poured through her and her pussy throbbed, aching to feel him again, her brain was too far gone to consider that point further. Right now all she could think about was the way his hands were touching her body, the feel of his growing arousal pressed against her abdomen. The way her mouth watered, thirsting for a taste of him.

"Well, I'm trying to get you naked so I can have my wicked way with you. It's only fair, don't you think? After all, you've seen me naked."

Hot. Wet. Needy. And naked.

His eyes smoldered, as if he was remembering every delicious detail of their erotic encounter.

Candace wet her lips, and he watched the action very carefully as his eyes moved over her face. Candace shifted her hips, positioning his cock right where she needed it as she gauged his reactions. His hard erection told her how much he wanted this, but would he hesitate or would he go for it?

"You know. A little tit for tat..." she added for good measure.

His laugh was edgy, churning with passion. His nostrils flared, and his jaw clenched like he was fighting some internal battle. Then something came over him, a shift of some sort, and he grabbed her hand. "Let's go."

"Go?"

"Yeah, you won, and winner takes all, remember?"

"Oh yeah. I remember." Candace's heart began to pound, as she was both excited and frightened by the intensity she'd spotted in his eyes.

Without preamble, Marc ushered them back to the inn, up the stairs and straight into the room. Once inside, she watched him close the door, set the lock and press his back to it. Candace drew a breath as excitement coiled through her veins. God, she hadn't seen such fervor in his eyes before. He tossed her a wild, predatory look and panned the length of her. "So tell me more about this tit for tat," he said, his voice husky with desire.

As moisture pooled between her thighs, she stepped back and ran her hands over the Tantra chair, wondering if he caught the sweet tang of her arousal. She lifted one eyebrow. "Have you used one of these before, Marc?" She pulled out the brochure and scanned the numerous positions, her hands trembling with need. "It's great for a thigh workout, if you're riding on top, that is."

The air around them charged, and her body quaked as she pictured herself on top of Marc, riding his cock with wild abandon. Then she took note of another possible position. Her

137

on her knees, Marc's cock in her mouth, and she knew exactly what she wanted to do first. She placed her hand on her stomach, where need gathered in a ball, and Marc's gaze shifted to her breasts.

Before she knew what was happening, he took charge and was on her, his hungry lips on hers, his hands moving over her body, pushing, pulling, giving and taking like he couldn't get enough of her. As much as she wanted him to take her again, pleasure her the way no other man ever had, she grabbed his hands and anchored them to his sides.

"Uh-uh. I'm the winner. I get to play it my way."

"You're only the winner because you cheated."

She put her hands on his abdomen, taking pleasure in his tight muscles, and grinned. "Such a sore loser."

"I'm not—"

Candace slipped her hand into his shorts and captured his cock, his words of protests suddenly forgotten, replaced by a heated moan. Now that she had him right where she wanted him—not a speck of hesitation on his face—she tugged at his shirt determined to find out if there could be more between them. If he was a man who could like her for who she was, because so far she liked everything about him.

She gestured with nod of her head. "I want these clothes gone, and then I want you to lie down on that chair for me. I'm in need of a thigh workout."

He brushed the back of his hands over her face and his touch went right through her. "Only if you let me undress you. I want you naked with me."

She sensed he was a man used to taking charge and taking care of others. But she wanted him to let his guard down with her so she could show him how good it was let someone take care of his needs. She was so used to men taking what they

138

wanted that until Marc she had no idea such giving, considerate men existed.

"Will you get naked with me, sweetheart?"

The vulnerability she heard in his voice tugged at her insides. When she nodded, he slipped his big rough hands under her shirt and slowly removed it, her bra quickly following. He then dropped to his knees and inched her shorts and panties down, his mouth so close to her skin she could feel his hot breath whispering over her thighs.

Once he had her naked, he stood, took a step back and just stared at her, his gaze caressing her body. "You're so damn sexy."

Candace quivered under his lusty glance, her breasts swollen, hot, aching to feel his mouth. But first, she wanted to taste him, to have her wicked way with him, the way he'd had it with her.

"You're still overdressed," she murmured seductively, loving the easy intimacy between them, the way she felt so comfortable with him as she stood there completely naked. There was no shyness, no awkwardness.

With that he made short work of his clothes and moved to the chair like she'd asked. He sprawled out, the curves shaping his hard athletic body. The position accentuated his washboard stomach, his firm thighs and his beautiful rock-hard cock, which was jutting out at her, clamoring for her undivided attention.

Muscles rippling, he reached for her. "Come here, sweetheart."

Instead of joining him on the chair, Candace kneeled on the floor before him and leaned forward. She rubbed her palms along the chair's soft suede fabric and pressed her breasts against it, stimulating her nipples. She wanted these next few minutes to be just about him.

His breathing grew shallow, and his deft fingers raced through her hair as his cock jolted. "Candace what—?"

"Winner takes all," she whispered before she closed her mouth over his cock, taking as much of him in as possible but knowing she'd never be able to *take all* where his impressive size was concerned.

As she worked her mouth up and down his cock, she tilted her head to see him. His dark eyes smoldered and his breathing hitched as he watched her. When her hair fell forward, he brushed it back and gave her a tender smile. Candace's heart fluttered, thrilled with the way he was studying her, concentrating on the action. Goodness, she really was an exhibitionist at heart.

She skated her tongue over his crown and tasted the pre-come on the tip. "Mmm."

Her moans of pleasure seemed to trigger a reaction. He fisted her hair and lifted his hips from the chair, powering upward as he chased an orgasm. His veins filled with blood and Candace could feel his pressure mounting. She greedily drew him in deeper, loving how he responded to her.

"Do you like that, baby? Do you like to suck my cock?"

Instead of answering she slipped her hand lower and cradled his balls. As her hand milked his rock-hard shaft, it occurred to her that being with him felt so intimate, so right. A riot of emotions erupted inside her, and she rocked forward, her pussy aching to feel him inside her.

His muscles spasmed, and as she continued to take pleasure in kissing and tasting him, she could sense his tension. When her fingers stroked over his beautiful cock, she could feel herself burning up, sparks shooting through her body. He gripped her hair and began to ease her off, but she shook her head, and continued to work her tongue over his tip while she ran her hand up and down the length of him, her other hand cupping and massaging his balls.

With single-minded determination, she made one more pass with her tongue, escalating his tension. A moment later his entire body tightened and he groaned. "Oh, Christ."

His cock tightened and contracted, then he erupted and Candace opened her mouth to drink in his salty sweetness. She stayed there for a long time, lapping up every last drop. Once he stopped spasming, she glanced up at him.

"Candace, sweetheart. Come here." The urgency and emotion in his voice made her tremble.

She slid up the chair until she was positioned over him. With her legs wrapped around his waist, she leaned forward, her breasts pressed against his moist chest. He drew her mouth to his, which brought them to an even deeper level of intimacy. His kiss was so full of emotion and tenderness it was all she could do to keep herself together. He lifted her higher and took one nipple into his mouth. As he laved her tight bud, he gripped her hips and moved them back and forth, rubbing her clit over his stomach, preparing her for him. She swallowed the lump in her throat, loving the way he was prepping her, concerned about her needs.

When he groaned, she reached behind her and touched his cock, excited to find it swollen and ready to go again. She inched away, needing him inside her more than she needed air, but he gripped her hips tighter and held her still.

Concerned eyes met hers. "You're not ready for me."

He slipped a hand between their bodies and brushed his thumb over her clit, his touch more emotional than physical. God, she couldn't believe how considerate he was. Honestly, he was too good to be true.

When his finger met with her drenched pussy, a moan of need sounded in her throat, and she threw her head back. He grinned, his soft chuckle washing over her. "So it seems you are ready." Then the smile fell from his mouth and something flitted over his face, something like pride, and he pitched his voice low. "I like how wet you get for me."

Frantic to feel him inside her, she tried to shimmy lower, but he held her and spoke in whispered words full of need. "Candace, sweetheart, slow down. We need a condom."

Cripes, she'd been so far gone, she hadn't stopped to consider it. "I don't—"

His cock probed her opening and he clenched his jaw. "I do, but my wallet is in the van."

Just then a noise on the windowsill gained their attention and they both turned. Abra jumped from his perch, and a box of condoms seemed to magically appear on the window shelf.

"When. How?" they said in unison.

Candace shook her head, perplexed at the oddness of it all but thankful for small miracles. "I don't know. But right now, I don't care." She climbed from the chair, crossed the room and grabbed the box of condoms. She removed one from the package, and as she placed it on the crown of his gorgeous cock, he never took his eyes off her, and his hands roamed her flesh, like he needed the intimate contact at all times. Once she completed sheathing him, she slid her leg around his waist, to position herself over his shaft. With her feet planted on the floor, she lowered herself, and his cock probed her pussy.

His fingers bit into her hips, and the passion that grew in his eyes nearly stopped her heart. She loved that he wanted her every bit as much as she wanted him. She bent forward and brushed her lips over his, the position of the chair enhancing intimacy between partners.

Abra purred and Marc asked in broken words, "Uh...Candace. Should we...put the cat out?"

"Yes," she whispered with effort, then sank down onto his cock, all thought of Abra forgotten.

Every ounce of bottled-up lust she had came rushing to the surface, and her need for Marc grew to insurmountable portions. She began bucking against him, riding him hard. His hands went to her nipples, where the soft pads of his thumbs circled her areolas. He spent a long time pleasuring her breasts before his big hands spanned her waist and held her tight.

Engulfed in desire, she pressed her palms to his chest and lifted herself up and down, up and down, driving his cock all the way inside her and reveling in the way his girth pressed against her walls and stroked the tiny bundle of nerves that made her delirious with want.

"You are so beautiful," he murmured, his voice rough, and when he bent forward to run his tongue over her nipples, a shudder overtook her. She gave a broken gasp and gripped his shoulders, bringing them chest to chest.

The rich scent of lovemaking curled around them, and Marc growled, his mouth finding hers. As he impaled her with his tongue, he cupped her buttocks and squeezed. Then his hand slipped around to the front where he stroked her with expertise. He parted her lips and sinuously circled her clit. Slow, torturous circles that nearly drove her mad with need. The man sure knew how to prolong a seduction.

As she shivered under his touch, she angled her body for deeper thrusts and her flesh moistened from the stab of pleasure. Her nails bit into his skin, and she pumped harder, her sex muscles tightening.

His eyes caressed hers with sultry heat. His gaze was dark, intense and unguarded. "Candace, baby. That's it, sweetheart, come for me," Marc encouraged, so in tune with her body and her every desire as he let down his shields and gave himself over to the pleasure.

She gave a throaty purr as a fine tremble moved through her. "So good..."

He pressed his finger harder against her clit and it obliterated all her control. Her soft quakes turned to heated tremors, and her body responded with a hot flow of release. She let herself go, giving herself over to Marc and to the pleasure he was bestowing upon her. As she tumbled into an orgasm, she bent forward and ran her teeth over his shoulder. He plunged deeper as her cunt pulsed and spasmed, her body going up in a burst of flames.

"Marc..." she cried out, completely lost in the sensation.

As she called his name, her cream dripped down his shaft, bathing him in her syrupy arousal. Then suddenly he stilled his movements, his dark turbulent eyes met hers as he let himself go. She squeezed her cunt, absorbing every delicious tremor, and he released inside her.

He pulled her in tight and she melted against him. They held each other for a long time, both breathing hard and gripping one another like their lives depended on it. A moment later she inched back and met his mouth. He kissed her deep, and her arms tightened around him, holding him impossibly closer. As she found solace in his embrace, his cock still buried inside her, she gave a contented sigh, deciding she never wanted to move, never wanted to break the intimate contact.

Marc shifted his mouth from hers to her neck to her ear and whispered, "That's one hell of a chair you got yourself here."

Candace gave an easy laugh. "Don't get too used to it."

He pulled back to see her and a perplexed look came over

his handsome face. "No?"

"Nope." She nodded toward the equipment still awaiting setup. "We've yet to try out the swing, and then there's the glider and the—"

His lips crashed down on hers, and her words were lost on a moan.

With that he took her again and again. Sometime throughout the night, they put the cat outside and made their way to the mattress, where he gathered her tight in his arms and covered them with a plush blanket. A wave of fulfillment and gratification came over her, but as she drifted off to sleep, one thought plagued her exhausted mind.

Marc Collins was too good to be true.

As sunlight poured into the room, Marc twisted sideways to take in the gorgeous sight before him. He sucked in a tight breath, hungering for her in ways that left him confused. He perused her naked body, his cock responding with interest. Oh fuck, he needed her again, needed her so much it left him dizzy. Needed her more than he'd ever needed anyone, or anything, in fact.

He touched her arm, trailing his hand over her silky skin. She moaned in her sleep, unconsciously rolling toward him in search of his touch, his heat.

Marc leaned forward and lightly brushed his tongue over her nipple, watching it harden and loving the way she responded to his mouth, even in sleep. Desire twisted his insides as he trailed lower, kissing and savoring her stomach and her bellybutton until he reached her pubis.

With delicious thoughts filling his mind, he eased her onto her back, inched open her thighs and climbed between. He braced a hand on either side of her hips and pressed his tongue to her pussy, brushing her clit ever so slightly and watching the way she writhed on the satin sheets.

So nice...

Blood pounded through his veins as he continued to indulge in her liquid heat. A moment later her hands raced through his hair and he darted a glance upward. "Good morning, sweetheart."

"Great morning," she murmured, looking lazy, rumpled, sexy and so damn satisfied his chest puffed with pride. She nudged his head, guiding him back down. Chuckling, he went back to tasting her sweetness, and she gave a whimper of delight in response.

He ravished her with his tongue, then slipped a finger inside. Her hips came off the mattress and he could tell by the small tremors that it wasn't going to take much to push her over. She was already incredibly aroused.

As her fingers played through his hair she drew a shaky breath. "Marc..."

"That's my girl." Her body tightened and she let herself go, creaming into his hungry mouth. "Mmm." He drank in every last drop.

When her tremors subsided, he slid up her body and hovered over her. A riot of emotions overcame him when he met her sleepy green eyes, and thought about the way she'd pushed him to let down his guard last night, to show him that he didn't always have to be in charge.

"Thanks for last night, sweetheart." Jesus, was that his voice? Just then he heard workers milling about outside and a wicked idea raced through his mind and brought on a tremble. It was his turn to play with her.

She smiled. "Thanks for this morning."

"Don't thank me just yet." He tossed her a mischievous grin and watched one sexy brow raise with intrigue.

"Marc?"

"Up," he demanded in a soft tone.

"What—?"

"There is something I want you to do for me."

Her eyes lit with interest, and her warm breath washed over him. "Oh yeah?"

"Yeah, you see that pole over there?"

Her gaze went from his face to the pole and she gave an excited gasp.

"I need you to show me something."

Her voice thinned to a whisper. "What's that?"

"Well, last night you showed me how to use the chair for exercise, so now I need to see how you use that pole. After all, if I'm going to be spending time in this room, I really should know how everything works, don't you think?"

Candace moistened her lips and her cheeks flushed pink as she slowly climbed from the mattress. "What I think is that you're a very bad boy." She made her way across the room, looking beautiful and naked and so alluring he nearly lost all coherent thought. As fierce possessiveness whipped through his blood, she wrapped one palm around the pole and swayed back and forth, her gorgeous breasts catching his attention.

Marc leaned back on the mattress, eager to take in the show. Warm early-morning sunlight poured in from the window and bathed her body in a golden glow. She lifted herself higher on the pole, wrapped her legs around it and slid downward. His cock throbbed to the point of pain as his eyes tracked down her body, taking in her lush softness and the way she pressed against that pole. Provocatively.

He cleared his throat. "You know, Candace, if anyone glances up here they'll see you."

She glanced toward the window and fire lit in her eyes. Working her way back up the pole, she turned her attention back to him, and the sultry, playful look on her face rattled his insides. As a burst of warmth rushed to his heart, he knew he was done for. Completely and utterly done for.

"Tell me. Did you position it in front of the window on purpose?"

"It's quite possible," she said in a breathless whisper.

He made a tsking sound and smiled at her, loving her honesty and her adventurous nature, but mostly loving the way she looked at him with pure adoration. "I think you're a very bad girl, Candace."

Her grin turned wicked, and he could hear the underlying question lacing her voice when she said, "Then that makes us quite the team."

It sure as hell did.

He looked into her eyes and saw need shining there. Intuition told him she felt the same way he did, but she was testing him, gauging his reactions as though wondering if there could be more between them. Sure they'd only recently met, but never had he reached such a deep level of intimacy or comfort with anyone before. It was as if some magical force had brought them together because they belonged to one another and were meant to be together forever.

Unable to take one more minute of her sexy act and needing to be inside her more than he needed to breathe, he climbed from the mattress, crossed the room and roughly pulled her to him. He jammed a leg between her thighs and felt her warm, wet pussy on his skin. Fuck, he loved how she was always ready for him. She locked her fingers together behind his head and kissed him long and deep.

She gyrated against his leg and he pressed against her harder, grinding his cock into her stomach. Beautiful expressive eyes met his and she poked him in the chest, fully aware of what he was up to. "Was that little show in front of the window for you or was it really for me?" There was so much emotion in her voice, it seeped under his skin and touched his soul.

His smile was as shaky as his hands as they raced over her. "Let's just say it was for both of us."

With that he lifted her ass, put her on the window ledge and pressed her back against the pane. "And so is this." He quickly sheathed himself, positioned his body between her spread legs and, with one powerful thrust, drove his cock all the way up inside her. "Sweet fuck," he murmured and knew he was in a heap load of trouble here.

He was crazy about Candace. She was fun and wild and adventurous, and unlike any woman he'd met before. He wanted her. All of her. And not just in the bedroom.

As her heat closed around him, he cupped her face and kissed her on the mouth. Hard.

What was it Pamina had said to him again? Sometimes things can get quite...*messy.* He'd made a mess of things all right. A big fucking mess. But Candace was so damn impossible to resist.

Regardless, he needed to make it right. For his sake and for Candace's.

Chapter Six

After Marc left her bedroom, assuring her he had business in the city to take care of, Candace descended the winding staircase in search of Pamina. Her mind raced, sorting through the whirlwind of events over the last few days.

They had a lot in common, but really she didn't know anything about him at all. Then again, he didn't know anything about her. Like him, she was vague when he questioned her about her family. Was he too hiding something? And what exactly was this business he had to take care of in the city?

Once again, *too good to be true* rushed through her mind.

When Candace reached the main level, Pamina came around the corner with Abra in her arms, his fur a tattered mess.

Candace furrowed her brow and took in his bedraggled state. "What the heck has he been up to?"

Pamina glared at Abra. "Nothing good, I can assure you of that."

Candace picked what looked like a chunk of brick mortar from his fur. "I think he needs a bath."

When Abra hissed at her, Pamina tapped his nose. "I definitely think a bath is in order and I don't care how much you dislike it."

As Pamina walked to the kitchen, Candace followed. "Pamina, I wanted to ask you about Marc."

With a squirming Abra tucked under her arm, Pamina grabbed two apples from the bowl and handed one to Candace. Candace polished it on her shirt then took a big bite.

"What about him?" Pamina asked, her mystical green eyes glistening.

"He's new in town and hasn't set up shop yet, so I was just wondering how you found him."

Pamina got quiet for a moment, thoughtful. "Well, he was walking toward the house the other day, and I assumed he was the paint stripper I'd hired. When I questioned him, he said he was the right man for the job." She gave a light chuckle, bit into her own apple. "Who knows? Maybe I accidentally hired the wrong guy. The wrong guy who happened to be in the right place at the right time. Just like he was in the right place at the right time when you needed a woodworker."

Candace swallowed hard as an uneasy feeling moved through her.

Pamina gave an easy shrug. "But what does it matter really? He's proven himself to be the perfect man for the job, don't you think?"

Yeah, in more ways than one.

"So who he is and where he's come from shouldn't matter, Candace. What matters is what he's done since he's been here."

Before she could comment, her cell phone rang and she excused herself.

Five minutes later, she hung up with her father. As she considered his tone, a knot settled into her stomach. There had been something in her father's voice that upset her. Although he'd assured her everything was fine, she sensed he was hiding something from her.

Deciding then and there that she needed to see him, she hopped into her car, drove to the station and boarded a train to Grand Central Station.

Marc paced outside Krane's office, catching glimpses of him talking to his secretary through his glass door. Jesus, what the hell was he supposed to say to him? Oh yeah, everything is going just fine, sir. Sure I've been keeping an eye on your daughter.

And a hand on her.

A tongue on her.

A cock in her.

Oh fuck!

He knew he was going to be out of a job, but none of that mattered to him. All that mattered was that he wanted to come clean with Candace so they could begin this relationship on the right foot and take it to the next level. If it wasn't too late for that. And the last thing he wanted was to be paid to take care of her. It was a job he'd happily do for free.

He just hoped Candace would understand and forgive him for his deceit.

A moment later Krane's door opened, and his secretary ushered him inside.

With Krane seated at his desk, Marc faced him straight on and said, "We need to talk."

Candace stepped off the elevator and moved through the marble foyer as she made her way to her father's office. Stepping up to Olive's desk, Candace greeted her with a smile.

Excited to see her, Olive rose from her chair and gave

Candace a hug. "Candace, how are you?"

Candace hugged her back. "I'm great. I was just in the area and I thought I'd stop in to see my father."

"He's with one of his security guards right now, but go on through. I'm sure he'll be happy to see you."

Candace slipped past Olive's desk and walked down the hall. As she neared her father's office, she took in the very familiar outline of the man with him, his legs wide, his back to the glass door. Candace's heart began to pound against her chest, and her knees went weak beneath her.

Oh good God, no.

She took a measured step closer, praying she was wrong but suspecting she wasn't. There was only one man she knew of who had that short military-cut hairstyle, broad shoulders that tapered to a trim waist and long powerful legs that she'd felt wrapped around her body. Intimately.

Her father looked past the man's shoulder and his eyes widened, surprised. But wait. Was that surprise that had registered on his face, or was it something else entirely?

The man with his back to the door—the security guard as Olive had identified him—angled his head and met her glance, confirming what she already knew. It was none other than Marc Collins.

As intense dark eyes met hers, she understood the look on her father's face because Marc was wearing the exact same expression. Guilt.

Candace felt her blood drain to her feet as understanding dawned. Her father had hired Marc to guard her without her knowledge. They'd both been deceiving her. She suddenly remembered an old conversation with her father after he'd been attacked on set, and how he'd hired and trained the set designer to be his guard. That had to have been Marc, seeing as

153

how he could so easily talk shop with her.

Every emotion from confusion to mortification to anger whipped through her blood as she spun around and rushed down the hall. Tears poured down her cheeks, blurring her vision. She could hear Marc chasing after her as she wiped the moisture from her eyes and hurried toward the waiting elevator.

Candace pressed the button and watched the metal ping shut, drowning out the noise and closing both the door and her heart to him. Numbly she tracked back to the train station, wanting to be as far away from Marc as possible. Sure, what her father had done was wrong, but at least he did it because he cared. What about Marc? He took the job to guard her because he was getting paid, and he jumped at the chance to be her woodworker simply to keep an eye on her. Was sleeping with her a fringe benefit, or was he getting paid for that too?

Her mind raced, trying to sort through the godawful turn of events as she boarded the train to Connecticut. Marc might not have been using her to get to her father, but he had been deceiving her, pretending to be someone he wasn't. Which made him no different from the other men who'd used her. She should have known he was too good to be true. The signs were there—the haircut, the way he moved, the way he continually scanned the area. But she had been too damn smitten to pay attention. Stupid. Stupid. Stupid.

A long while later Candace made her way to the inn, both physically and mentally drained. With her emotions in a tangled mess, she needed to be alone, to come to terms with everything that had happened. As she entered the front door and made her way to the staircase, she wondered why the hell she'd broken the pact she'd made with her best friends—to stay away from all men. Hadn't lessons learned long ago taught her anything?

She put her foot on the first stair, but the sound of Marc's voice behind her stilled her movement.

"Candace, wait."

Her whole body tightened, and she wrapped her arms around herself, not wanting to hear any more lies from him. "I think you should go."

"I think you need to hear what I have to say." The emotions in his voice made her heart clench.

She spun to face him and bit out, "Why do I need to hear what you have to say? I don't even know who you are."

"Yes, you do, Candace. Everything between us is real."

The pained look on his face touched her deeply, and the soft tone of his voice spoke of sadness and distress, and made it so damn difficult to keep hold of her anger. "How can I believe that?"

"I never meant to hurt you," he admitted. She was astonished by the sincerity and tenderness in his tone. "I wanted to tell you who I was, and I tried to keep my distance from you, but I couldn't. I wanted you so much I just couldn't fight it anymore." His hands clenched at his sides and she could see the way his breathing had changed, become harder, more erratic.

She suddenly remembered the conflict in his eyes. The hesitation. Had he been trying to pull back, to fend off her advances? Honestly, what chance did he have? There was no denying the attraction between them was palpable, and with the way she'd been teasing and tormenting him, she'd made it impossible for him to fight the attraction. Perhaps she too carried some of the blame.

"I went to your father's office to quit, Candace."

That caught her by surprise. "You quit?"

"Yes."

"Why?"

"Because I don't want money to protect you. That's a job I'd gladly do for free."

She gulped air. "You can't just quit. What are you going to do? Where will you work?"

"I don't know. Working here with you has reminded me how much I love to use my hands. How much I miss set design and woodworking. Maybe I will set up that shop after all."

"What about all your training as a security guard? You're going to let that go to waste?"

"Not a chance, because if you'll let me, I'd like to spend the rest of my life protecting you."

Her heart leapt, aware of what he was asking of her. She planted her hands on her hips, not ready to let him off the hook just yet, but deep in her heart knowing she would. Because he was warm and kind and loving and gentle. A fiercely protective man who gave without taking, and to her that spoke volumes. He was a man who'd made a mistake and was now suffering every bit as much as she was. "Who says I need protection?"

"I do." He stepped closer and brushed his thumb over her cheek. "You father has enemies, Candace, and I plan on making sure none of them ever finds or touches you."

As she leaned into him, absorbing the heat from his hand, she knew he truly was sorry and hadn't intentionally hurt her. In that instant she felt her anger melt and thought more about what Pamina had to say. Pamina might have mistaken him for someone else, but there was no doubt that he was right guy at the right time. And forget about too good to be true. This guy was good. Great, in fact. And he was true, honest and giving. Not to mention the best thing that had ever happened to her. It also occurred to her that she didn't feel smothered by him or his protective nature. She felt loved and cherished.

He must have sensed the shift in her because he pulled her tight. "But the only question is, who's going to protect you from me?"

She pressed against him and chuckled. "Uh, do you have something in your pocket or are you just happy to see me?"

He laughed. "I picked something up for you while I was in the city today." Sadness crossed his eyes. "Then I was worried you'd never speak to me again, and I'd never get the chance to give it to you." He reached into his pocket and pulled out a new iPod. "After all, I was responsible for damaging yours in the first place."

Warmth moved through her as she recalled their seductive encounter at the lake. "You really are one of a kind, aren't you?"

He turned serious. "Candace, I really am sorry I never told you who I was. I don't want there to be any secrets between us."

"We can put that behind us, Marc." Once again she recalled the mystical Pamina's words. "What matters is what you've done since you've been here. And what you've done is opened my eyes and shown me what love really is." With that she grinned and held her hand out. "I'm Candace Steele and I'm an interior designer. I'm also the daughter of Jason Krane, famous New York movie director. Oh, and I've recently discovered I'm a regular old exhibitionist."

Marc covered her hand with his and visibly relaxed. "I'm Marc Collins, set designer turned security guard for Jason Krane, famous New York movie director. And I'm totally in love with his daughter. Oh, and I'm a regular old voyeur."

Candace laughed out loud, the love she felt for him filling her darkest corners. "Then that makes us quite the team."

"That's right Candace, we do make a good team, and always know this, that I love you for who you are."

Her heart soared. *He loved her.* "I love you too."

"Come with me."

"Where are we going?"

"To the bedroom."

Desire moved through her. "Oh, yeah."

"There are some other things we need to square up."

"Like what?"

"Well, like this." He pulled her tight and pressed his cock against her. "And since you had your wicked way with me this morning..."

Candace smiled and wet her mouth, knowing full well it was Marc who'd had his wicked way with her that morning. "So what exactly are you suggesting. A little tit for tat?"

"I believe I might be, Candace. I believe I just might be."

All Lit Up

Dedication

Too my wonderful editor, Anne, who always helps me shine
and is a dream to work with.

Chapter One

Now that had to be the most scrumptious ass Anna Deveau had ever set eyes on.

Tight.

Defined.

And downright squeezable.

The warm autumn sun beat down on Anna as she swiped her tongue over her dry bottom lip and zeroed in on the delectable male before her. Cripes, that man had buttocks like none other. Firm, ripe, ready for the picking.

Oh my...

As a shiver of awareness tingled deep between her legs, derailing her hard-fought ability to think straight, Anna took extra care in negotiating the cracked and pitted walkway in her thin-soled flip-flops.

Pamina kept pace beside her—the mystical-like woman who'd hired Anna's firm to create fantasy-inspired theme rooms in the rundown Victorian inn situated on the outskirts of Mason Creek. As they strolled along the dilapidated path, Lindsay, a childhood friend and fellow colleague, caught up with them, and they all made their way to the masonry van in the driveway—where said scrumptious buns stood waiting. With the back doors spread wide open, Mr. Sex in a Pair of Jeans braced his muscular thighs against the bumper and leaned forward, presenting her with a perfect, unobstructed view of his magnificent backside.

Yummy...

His gluteus maximus muscles were perfect, all right. Perfect for pinching, or grabbing hold of and palming while he made sweet passionate love to her. A romantic at heart, Anna envisioned those strong hands of his removing her clothes, slowly, methodically, taking the utmost care with her body. Her thighs quivered as she gifted herself a moment to play out the sexy scenario—gentle fingers touching her private, intimate parts with purpose, the rough pad of his thumb working her sensitive nub into orgasmic bliss, his warm, wet mouth buried in the crook of her sensitive neck as he whispered sweet nothings in her ear. A small rapturous moan threatened to crawl out of her throat, and she promptly choked it back as the erotic slideshow played out in her mind's eye.

Taking her by surprise, small beads of moisture broke out on her forehead, and she swiped at them, but the dampness had nothing at all to do with the hot sunshine beating down on the quaint town, and everything to do with the pact she'd made with her friends. A pact she was suddenly questioning the intelligence of. Damn, it had been so long since she'd engaged in an intimate relationship that her body had turned mutinous. Deep between her legs she felt libidinous, needy and hungry.

Positively horny.

Which had her questioning the logic behind their pact, and begged the question—exactly why had they all renounced the opposite sex again?

"What do you think, Anna?" Pamina asked.

Anna turned toward the tall, willowy woman with the knowledgeable green eyes, and struggled to comprehend the question. As Pamina stared at her, obviously awaiting a response, she shifted Abra—her very overweight cat—in her long, lithe arms as the ornery feline hissed and swatted at an imaginary fly.

Lindsay shot her a questioning glance. "Yeah, what is your opinion on it, Anna?" Her friend's brow furrowed in concentration as she carefully picked her way forward in a pair of three-inch spiked heels that only a wild brazen woman like Lindsay could pull off.

Not understanding the question and feeling a bit flustered by the sexual energy zinging through her bloodstream, Anna tucked a short blonde lock behind her ear and blinked her mind into focus.

"Anna?" Lindsay asked again.

Just then one of the many skilled workers on assignment at the inn crossed in front of her, and she nearly bumped into him.

"I, uh." Goodness she'd been so caught up in lusting after Mr. Sex in a Pair of Jeans, completely preoccupied with the delicious images of his hard body climbing over hers, that she hadn't been paying any attention to their conversation, or to all the other laborers milling about in an effort to return the inn to its natural, beautiful state. Truthfully, it was hard to believe that the mere sight of a hot guy had the ability to render her senseless. She was a smart woman, logical, proper, always maintaining a professional demeanor at the workplace, so what had suddenly gotten into her? What the heck had her thinking wayward thoughts about a man she didn't even know?

Lack of sex, she supposed.

No doubt it would shock her friends if they discovered the naughty direction her thoughts had taken. Not that she would tell them. When it came to sex, unlike the bold and vivacious

Lindsay, Anna was a very private person. Then again, she shouldn't be fantasizing about the laborer Pamina had hired in the first place. It was a distraction she didn't need. Especially since time was of the essence. She'd put so much work into perfecting her design that she was just beginning the renovations and Lindsay and Anna were well on their way to finishing.

From her peripheral vision, she spotted Candace, the third and final partner in their bustling interior-decoration business, Styles for Living. Candace lunged forward, stretching her muscles on the sun-crisped lawn before her habitual early-morning run. Thankful for the distraction, and deciding to take the focus off her and her current lack of communication skills, Anna gave a wave and shouted a friendly greeting. Pamina and Lindsay fixed their gazes on Candace and followed suit.

After exchanging pleasantries, Anna turned her concentration back to negotiating the walkway. Fortunately for her, Pamina and Lindsay returned to their conversation, forgetting all about Anna's opinion. Deciding to pay a little more attention, she half listened to them discuss Lindsay's BDSM room, but Mr. Sexy proved too much of a distraction, and Anna stole another glance as they closed the distance between them.

As though unaware of their presence as they approached his van, Mr. Sexy ripped off his professional polo shirt, the company name embroidered on the back, and proceeded to change into his work wear. Good Lord! His sun-kissed skin was bronzed, smooth and glistening under the morning rays. Firm shoulders tapered to a trim waist and the delectable sight had her feeling all warm and wicked inside. A fine tingle worked its way down her body and loitered around that hungry little spot between her legs. If the mere sight of his backside had the ability to rattle her like dice in a Yahtzee cup, she could just imagine what a full frontal would do to her.

Truthfully, only one other guy had ever made her feel so edgy, so sexually aroused, and she hadn't set eyes on him since high school. Nor did she have any desire to. Not after what he'd done to her. Which suddenly reminded her why she'd agreed to the pact and sworn off men in the first place. She frowned, then quickly buried those thoughts in favor of more pleasant ones.

No, it certainly wasn't the time to dredge up old painful memories of Daniel Long, the cute boy next door and Mason Creek High School sports hero who'd been coveted by all. It was time to take pleasure in the fit man before her and commit every striated muscle to memory. At least then when she was lying in bed later that night, it would give her something to fantasize about while she took the edge off. And take the edge off she would. Just because she'd sworn off men and had given up on finding her very own Prince Charming, didn't mean she couldn't dream about delicious, orgasmic sex, did it?

She absently toyed with the gold chain around her neck, bit back a chuckle and shook her head. To think that just a short while ago, she'd been both shocked and embarrassed as she stood on the sidewalk outside Toys4Gals and examined the array of sexual devices through the curbside window. Never had she thought she'd purchase such a toy, let alone use one. Now, here she was gathering quite the collection in her bedside table. Working solo wasn't normally her style. But lack of action had forced her to think outside the box—or inside the box—or... Oh hell, she didn't know what she was thinking anymore. All she knew was that she was hurting. Anna gave a quick shake of her head to clear her salacious musings and wondered if a quick shake of her hips would help push back the lust that gathered there.

As she tried to marshal her thoughts and focus on the job at hand, Pamina stepped forward and spoke to the man at the rear of the truck. Mr. Sex in a Pair of Jeans turned to face the woman who'd hired him. With his work shirt dangling in his left hand, he reached out with his right. As they exchanged greetings, Anna shot him a glance. Catching his profile, she began a leisurely inspection of his perfect physique. So much for her efforts to redirect her concentration.

Beginning with his rock-hard thighs, she let her glance wander upward, stopping to linger around that impressive bulge just below his waistband. A tremble worked its way through her body and her mind went on an erotic journey as her gaze climbed higher, to take in his handsome face and chiseled features. When her eyes met his, he angled his body, giving her a full-frontal view. As Anna took in the Grade A specimen at the back of the truck, her brain practically shut down and her jaw gaped open. It couldn't be.

Oh God, it just couldn't be.

She attempted to speak, but couldn't seem to formulate any words as the sight of the man standing before her left her speechless.

Totally and utterly speechless.

Not because of those long hewn legs of his, or how she envisioned them wrapped around her body. Not because her fingers itched to touch those tight sculpted abdominals, now damp with early-morning perspiration. And definitely not because those mesmerizing hazel eyes seemed to be staring into her soul, unearthing feelings best left buried.

Oh no, not at all. It was because the man behind those eyes was none other than Daniel Long, the high-school stud who'd destroyed her belief in Prince Charming and happily-ever-after.

He gave her a wolfish grin, flashing his perfect white teeth, as he took one measured step closer, closing the small gap between them. He dipped his head and put his mouth close to hers, and his warm breath felt more intimate than a kiss. As her body absorbed the heat radiating off his bare chest, her nipples tightened beneath her cotton sundress, and she crossed her arms over her chest, fearing he could see her ill-favored arousal.

He gave her a warm smile and a moment of silence ensued as she took a brief second to peruse the features of the man before her. Gone was the young handsome boy from high school and in his place existed a man. A real man. Tall, broad and oozing sensuality in a way the young Daniel never had. The years had definitely done him well, she decided.

"Hi, Anna." His sensuous tone curled through her body like an aphrodisiac as his familiar scent thickened her blood. Not only did that provocative aroma take her back in time, it aroused her senses and made her feel downright hot.

Edgy and distracted, her every nerve ending burned with unfettered desire. Her legs went a little rubbery and she locked her knees to keep herself upright. Once again silence hung heavy, and the tortured sound of her swallowing down the lump that had taken up residency in her throat cut through the air.

Striving for normalcy, Anna blinked her eyes tight and opened them again, convinced that she was hallucinating. Surely lack of sex had her mind conjuring up images of the guy she'd lusted after for years, because no way could her high school crush—captain of the football team and every girl's dream—be standing before her. Years previous Daniel had gone off to the city for college, and the last place she expected to see him was here in Mason Creek, Connecticut, standing behind a masonry truck, no less. As she sorted through matters, one question remained. Why had he come back after all these years?

He gave a sexy tilt of his head, his eyes assessing her. "It's nice to see you again." His voice was dark and warm, his tone husky and sensual just like she'd remembered, and despite herself, she leaned into him, momentarily forgetting past hurts.

But the ever-protective Lindsay hadn't forgotten. Not even for a minute. She cupped Anna's arm and hauled her back. Her eyes shot daggers at Daniel when she said, "I think you should leave."

Daniel continued to stare at Anna, but with her brain currently on overdrive, trying to process this unexpected turn of events, she could barely vocalize a response.

Deep smoldering eyes skated over her. "Do you want me to leave, Anna?" She didn't miss the invitation or the odd ache of longing in his voice. Nor did she miss the strange way he was looking at her.

"Do you?" he asked again.

As her brains screamed yes, her body, especially the moist juncture between her legs, screamed no. No with a capital N.

"Daniel—" she croaked out, not really knowing what she was about to say.

Discretion aside and ignoring those around them, he touched her hair and that intimate gestures spread warmth through her body. "It's been a long time."

"Yeah, a long time," she agreed, shocked that she could actually speak, let alone formulate a sentence.

"Too long." Something in his voice hitched and Anna had the distinct feeling that he wasn't at all surprised to see her, and that, unlike her, he was completely prepared for this encounter.

Was it possible that it was she who'd inspired him to come home?

She quickly dismissed that ridiculous notion as soon as it

hit, and resisted the urge to slap her forehead. Good God, she'd spent years trying to get over him, and it irked her that all it took was one second in his presence to have her fantasizing about Prince Charming and happily-ever-after again. With him. Him! The guy who only thought of her as a conquest, one of a handful of high school girls he'd yet to nail. Perhaps he'd come back to try again. At that thought, Anna squared her shoulders and pulled herself together. Well he could forget it. He couldn't get into her panties back then and he certainly wasn't about to now.

"Of course she wants you to leave," Lindsay interjected and jerked her thumb out toward the road.

Feeling much more in control than she had seconds before, Anna touched Lindsay on the shoulder. "It's okay. I've got this."

"You sure?"

"Yes. Just give us a minute." With that both Lindsay and Pamina stepped aside, but not far enough that they couldn't hear their conversation, or Lindsay couldn't intervene if she felt Anna needed her assistance.

Anna turned to Daniel. He'd only been a boy when he'd given her a hard cold dose of reality, a boy who cared about his own needs. Thankfully she'd found out what he was all about before she'd handed her heart over to him. Because once she had, she was sure there'd have been no coming back from that. In fact, maybe she should be thanking him for opening her eyes to the real world, where Prince Charming existed only in Disney movies and romance novels.

"Why are you here, Daniel?"

He gestured with a nod toward the two women hovering nearby. "I was hired by Pamina to install marble around the Jacuzzi tub and to lay brick around the fireplace."

Anna gave a quick shake of her head. "No, what I mean is

why are you here? In Mason Creek. I thought you'd moved away for good."

He grew quiet for a moment, as if weighing his words carefully, then stated the obvious, "I'm back."

"I can see that." She tapped a restless foot. "What I want to know is why?"

Warm heat passed over his eyes. "Because I—" He opened his mouth to tell her, then seemed to change his mind. He gave a casual shrug and in a low, controlled voice said, "I thought it was time."

"Last I heard you hated Mason Creek, and everything about it. And when you went off to college, you had no intentions of ever coming back."

He drew back looking a little hurt, like her words had triggered some dark memory. "I'm helping my brothers with their business."

Anna nodded. She'd completely forgotten that his older brothers had started the town's only masonry business, very much needed now, thanks to the growth in the housing market and the boom in new home construction. But hadn't Daniel gone to State college to get a business degree? Not that she was keeping tabs on him. Because she wasn't. Not really.

"It's crazy how much they've expanded," he added.

As she listened, she wondered what a guy with a business degree knew about masonry work.

"I take care of the office end of things," he said, answering her unasked question. Then he grinned and laughed fondly under his breath. "Mike and John have made a mess of the paperwork. Good thing I came back when I did."

Anna crossed her arms. "If you run the business end, then what do you know about laying marble and bricking around a fireplace?"

"I'm not without my own skills." He paused, then pitched his voice low. "I can do a good job for you, Anna. I promise. I'll make it good. Real good."

She swallowed hard and wondered if he was talking about laying marble or something else entirely.

Lindsay stepped in, probably catching his sexual undertones as well. "I don't think you're the man for the job."

He shrugged. "I'm all you've got." He gestured toward the house. "We're the only game in town, so if you want the work done..."

"Send someone else from the company."

"My brothers are on other jobs. Completely buried." When he turned his mesmerizing hazel eyes on her, it felt like she'd been sucker-punched. "I'm your man, Anna."

The way he'd said those four simple words caused the blood in her veins to boil. Years ago, she'd really thought he was her man. So sweet, kind, respectful and genuine. Confident, yet always a little shy around her. A real-life Prince Charming. But it was all an act to get her into his bed. She'd learned long ago that beneath that perfect package, Daniel Long was nothing but a bad apple.

And no matter how much he charmed her she would never, ever sleep with him.

She didn't think.

Daniel watched her—watched the way her telltale opaque blue eyes had raked over his body with heated interest, her flesh moistening from want—only to turn around and see lust give way to anger when their glances collided and recognition hit like a wrecking ball.

What had he ever done to make her hate him?

That question that had plagued him for years. A question that had finally forced him to leave his high-paying job in the city and return home to Mason Creek. With the help of his brothers, he'd kept close tabs on Anna and her family over the years. After all, as teens they'd all been neighbors, and to this day, their parents still shared a backyard.

Truthfully, it was fate that he'd come back when he had. Shortly after arriving, Pamina had contracted their company for a job, which meant Daniel had to learn how to do masonry work and learn how to do it fast. A crash course later, here he was, standing face to face with the woman who'd tormented his soul since he'd moved in next to her during his senior year of high school.

In all the years that he's been gone, he'd yet to get her out of his mind. And no matter how many women he'd bedded, he couldn't help but imagine he was holding the sweet girl from next door. The same girl who'd always reduced him to a bumbling idiot whenever she was near.

Many years ago, the first sight of her face had pretty much ruined him for any other woman. Lord knows he'd tried for the distraction. After skipping town he'd slept with anything in a skirt, but all that proved was that his heart belonged at home, with Anna. She was smart, modest and romantic, so unlike the other girls he knew. He grinned, thinking about how many times he'd spied on her from his bedroom window, watching her indulge in one of her romance novels, or put together designs in her sketch book while she lounged on her back deck.

Back in high school, the girls had thrown themselves at him. Daniel had been captain of the football team, and everyone had wanted a piece of him. He could have had any girl he wanted, but the one girl he really longed for, the one who lived next door, was the one girl he couldn't have.

Now he was back, no longer that nervous young boy he once was, ever determined to prove how good they could be together. She might hate him, for reasons he vowed to unveil, but he'd be damned if she didn't want him. The desire in her eyes reflected his own and spoke volumes. They both had it bad for each other, and he was hell-bent on doing something about it.

As she stood there staring up at him, her blue eyes glistening beneath the early-morning rays, his heart did a little flip. The warmth in her gaze had never failed to affect him and just being this close to her had his brain swirling with need.

She felt that need every bit as much as he did. It was written all over her face; her eyes were full of want, her body full of unrequited longing. But she continued to turn a blind eye to it, ignoring the powerful chemistry between them, just like she had in high school, when she'd suddenly stopped speaking to him.

Sure he'd tried to speak with her, to figure out what had gone wrong, but every time he'd made an attempt, her protective friend Lindsay came between the two. Anna had stopped coming to the backyard fence to chat with him, and had distanced herself by staggering the time she left for school. Daniel had wanted to set things straight, but he was so young and insecure with her, and things had gotten so awkward he'd had no idea how to close the ever-expanding gap.

As he sorted through matters, he reflected on the emotions she brought out in him, the emotions he brought out in her. Oh yeah, it was well past the time to set the wheels into motion and go after what he wanted. He was no longer that shy boy and had every intention of peeling away her layers and discovering the truth, and in the process teaching her how right they were for each other, because he didn't just want her in his bed, he wanted her in his life.

When he was done with her, not only would she acknowledge the heat between them, she'd willingly act on it, giving herself over to him completely and utterly, body and soul, begging him to fulfill her every need, her every aching desire. Then he'd prove once and for all that they were meant to be together, and they could start making up for lost time.

He stepped closer, close enough that he could feel a tremble move through her body, and dipped his head.

He cleared his throat and lowered his voice for her ears and her ears only. "So what do you say, Anna?"

Simmering blue eyes flitted over him and he could see the torment on her face, the need, the want, the uncertainty. He fisted his hands and resisted the urge to haul her body against his and press his lips to hers, anxious to explore her mouth, her breasts, between her legs, anxious to finally introduce himself to every inch of her body the way he'd longed to do for years.

"Do you want me or not?"

Dark lashes blinked over smoldering blue eyes. "I...want you."

He let out a breath he didn't realize he was holding, and his heart settled back into a steady rhythm. He took in her watchful eyes and said, "Then lead the way."

Chapter Two

With Daniel tight on her heels, Anna could barely walk, let alone breathe. Good Lord, if she couldn't put one foot in front of the other, how the heck was she supposed to paint walls, sew curtains and stuff down feathers into the throw cushions? She was liable to lose her mind, not to mention her resolve, with Daniel—shirtless, no less—in such confined quarters with her.

Just thinking about him on his knees, bent over that lover's tub, all hard muscles and sinewy brawn flexing, rippling and relaxing again, had her nipples hardening, pressing against her thin dress and arousing her even more. What she'd do to fill that tub with bubbles and scented rose petals and haul him inside with her. By small degrees her body tightened and ribbons of pleasure forked through her. Deep between her thighs, her sex moistened, dampening her cotton panties. Anna pulled her sundress around her legs and prayed he couldn't smell her arousal as it saturated the long hallway.

Okay, so she couldn't deny that he was handsome, charming and charismatic, and she wasn't at all immune to his blatant sexuality. But that didn't mean she was just going to jump into bed with him, even though everything in the way he looked at her, everything in his body language, spoke of physical want and desire. Sure she wanted him to want her, but not because she was the one girl he couldn't nail. She wanted him to like her for who she was, and for what she was all about.

She cast a glance over her shoulder and he seemed to be lost in his own thoughts.

Trying for casual but failing miserably, she instructed, "Please put your shirt on." She cringed. Damn she'd blurted that out with much more angst than she meant.

His brow rose a fraction. "Right. My shirt," he said, his voice distant, obviously distracted. What the heck was he thinking about anyway?

After he pulled his blue, short-sleeved and form-fitting work shirt on, he stepped up beside her and they passed by Candace's room. Daniel glanced in. He made a face when he spotted the Tantra chair. "What kind of rooms are you designing anyway?"

"Whatever we want. Pamina left it up to each of us. I'm pretty excited about it actually."

"What kind of room has a Tantra chair and a floor-to-ceiling pole?"

"The kind that combines sex and exercise."

He chuckled and the sound went right though her. "Ah, I should have known. Candace always was into fitness."

"Lindsay's designing a BDSM room." She shot him a glance to gauge his reaction, fully expecting the wild and wicked Daniel, a big alpha male who enjoyed the conquest, to be intrigued by such a thing.

"I guess I can see her into that kind of thing." He shrugged and seemed less impressed than she'd thought he'd be. A slow grin curled his mouth when he added, "And I see she's *still* overly protective of you."

Anna returned his smile. "That's my Lindsay." As she pushed open her bedroom door, his words sank in. "You seem to remember an awful lot about my friends."

Not that she'd forgotten anything about him. She recalled it all, in fact. From their private backyard conversations, their long walks to school, to the sweet-sixteen party that she'd purposely excluded him from. And of course, she'd never forget the eye-opening conversation she'd heard between him and his friends the week before said party.

Instead of answering, he probed, "So we have an athletic room, a BDSM room..." He paused, giving her an opening.

"For my room—"

He cut her off. "Let me guess. A room for the romantically inclined."

Anna studied him, and for a brief second she thought she spotted a little-boy-lost look. Something inside her stomach tightened. She remembered that look of vulnerability, had witnessed it many times when they were teens and had spoken to one another over the backyard fence, when he would stumble over his words and make her feel all weird and special inside. But it had all been an act, right? He was simply the confident quarterback out to win at all costs.

One strong hand slipped around her side and came to rest on the small of her back as he guided her to the door. At first touch sexual energy arced between them. The feel of his warm palm on her flesh did the most delicious things to her insides, and she bit down on her bottom lip, trying to fight off the overwhelming desire she had for him.

He dipped his head and positioned it close to her ear. "After you," he murmured.

As she moved through the doorway, he gave her a smile so sweet and genuine her insides twisted, and she took a moment to consider things longer. Time had changed him outwardly, for the better, could it have changed him inwardly as well? Did he remember things about her and her friends because he'd grown up, changed his ways? Taking an interest in more than just his next conquest?

"So how'd you guess I was designing a romantic room for lovers?"

He cocked a brow. "A Jacuzzi tub. A fireplace. It's pretty obvious."

Okay, so it *was* pretty obvious, proving he didn't really know *her* or her desires at all.

"Right. Of course." She rolled her eyes and berated herself for her wishful thinking.

"What?"

"Nothing."

"Then why did you roll your eyes?"

"I was just thinking some things never change."

His voice was a low, strained whisper when he countered, "And here I was just thinking some things should."

Anna gulped. She didn't miss the sexual undertones or his undisguised need, nor was she unaffected by the deep-seated desire she heard in his voice. But she was *not* going to sleep with him, no matter how hard he tried to seduce his way into her panties. Decision made, she pushed back her lust, stepped away from him and his warm body, and waved her hand around the room.

Daniel followed her gaze, and she watched him take in the big bay window overlooking the pond, as well as the old fireplace that was in need of an updated design. She grabbed her sketchbook off the nightstand and stepped toward the bathroom door.

"The Jacuzzi tub is in here."

Daniel moved in behind her and pressed his chest to her

back. He glanced over her shoulder and looked at the sketchpad. "These are your ideas?"

She angled her head to see him and when he gave a low side-to-side shake of his head, she tilted her chin, ready to defend her artistic designs. "Yes. They're my ideas."

"They're fantastic." He scrubbed a hand over his jaw and a look of genuine respect crossed his face. "This room is going to be spectacular. I can't wait to see the end product."

She felt pride well up inside her. She'd worked hard on her designs, and although she appreciated his enthusiasm and confidence in her, she mostly hated that it meant so much to her.

His grin was slow, if not a little wicked, and arousal edged his voice. "A woman doesn't stand a chance if a guy brings her here."

"What do you mean?" Trying to see the room from his eyes, she perused the large space, taking in the king-sized bed with the unfinished white down duvet still haphazardly thrown over it, the jasmine-scented candles which she'd yet to strategically position for romance and ambiance, and the maroon-colored walls used to enhance passion and imagination, and awaken the romantic spirit in one's lover.

"With this romantic ambiance, a woman will easily fall under her man's spell, don't you think?"

"That's what I'm going for. Romance and Prince Charming might not be in the cards for me, but I'm hoping it will inspire it for someone else." When she caught the odd look on his face she knew she'd said too much and immediately began to backpedal, stumbling over her words. "I...uh...I...mean—"

"I always knew you had talent, Anna." He gave her a way out and she appreciated the gesture more than he knew.

She wrinkled her nose, unprepared for the mix of emotions

she suddenly felt. "You did. How?"

A sheepish look crossed his face—a sweet innocent look she'd only ever seen him give her—and it knotted her all up inside and affected her in the most bizarre ways. What the heck was it about that unguarded expression of his that always got to her, anyway? Not wanting him to know her true feelings, she pinched herself, a quick reminder that it was all an act. Right?

Anna pressed. "How, Daniel? How did you know I had talent?"

"Back in high school, I saw some of your designs." He rolled on the balls of his feet, swaying back and forth like a schoolboy who got caught with his hand in the cookie jar.

She furrowed her brow in thought. "I never showed you any of my designs."

"I used to see them when you sat in the backyard with your sketchbook," he confessed.

Her lids widened, and she tucked a strand of hair behind her ear. "You were spying on me."

"Well technically it wasn't spying." He gave her a half-smile and continued. "My bedroom window overlooked—"

"You were. You were spying on me." Probably so he could learn things about her and sweet-talk his way into her pants.

Penetrating eyes full of desire and seduction met hers. His tongue snaked out to moisten his lips and in a swift move, he grabbed her hips and pulled her close. The warmth of his touch traveled all the way to the tips of her toes, igniting her flesh along the way. Her body turned to mush and she could feel herself blushing. Hazel eyes smoldered with passion, and something else. Something dark and intense that Anna couldn't quite put a name to.

His gaze fixed on her mouth. "Anna, I—"

She wanted him. God, how she wanted him. On the bed, up against the wall, down on the floor and inside the tub. She ached to feel those strong arms around her waist. To have that warm wet mouth on her body, and to finally experience what so many other women before her had—the pleasure of his cock moving in and out of her and bringing her joy beyond anything she'd ever known. Oh bloody hell, she needed this so badly her entire body shuddered in anticipation. A fire she knew better than to let burn free ignited between her legs. A reminder that she was a woman and standing before her was a red-blooded man who could undoubtedly satisfy all her unsatiated needs.

So what was she going to do about it?

Just then Abra came sauntering into the room. His loud purr had her mind reeling back to reality. With trembling fingers, she pressed the sketchpad into Daniel's stomach and pushed past him, desperate for a reprieve. It was time to get her head on straight and start concentrating on the job at hand. "We have a schedule to follow so it's time to get to work. Pamina wants to open the inn as soon as possible and I'm falling behind. I'll leave you to look over the plans and if you have any questions, I'll be downstairs."

Or in a cold shower trying to take the edge off.

With that Anna left the room. Once outside she sagged against the wall and clutched her stomach as she drew a rejuvenating breath. Goodness, the man still got to her in a way no other man could, stirring things deep inside her and leaving her warm and wanting. Spending a week in the same room with him was going to play havoc with her libido. If she didn't soon pull herself together she just might do something she'd regret later—like go back in there, rip his clothes off, and answer the demands of her body once and for all. But since she wasn't into casual sex, and "wham bam thank you, ma'am" wasn't her style, she had to find another way to tamp down her desires—

heartbreak wasn't an option.

But if he kept using sexual undertones when he spoke to her, how the hell was she going to resist? Clearly he wanted her physically as much as she wanted him. Was she simply fighting the inevitable?

Daniel worked to rein in his lust as he watched her sashay out the door. Her firm, lush ass dragged his focus and made breathing damn near impossible. His plan was to seduce her, but truth be told, just being around her reduced him to a hormonal teenager again. Hadn't he left that shy young boy behind when he went off to college? Honestly the heat between them had instantly leveled him to that high school bumbling idiot again and rattled him to his very core.

Still, regardless of the sparks between them, she ignored it. Since time was of the essence and the job wouldn't take much more than a week, he had to amp up the seduction and melt her resolve. Once she handed herself over to him, he'd show her how good it could be between them. Then there'd be no turning back. Now, only one question remained. What was the best way to go about seducing the sweet and romantic Anna?

As he watched her go, he replayed their conversation in his mind, desperate to understand everything about her, from what drove her professionally to what made her tick personally. Sure he'd known Anna as a teen, but now he wanted to know Anna as a woman. Her needs, desires, likes and dislikes.

A noise outside the door gained his attention, and he hoped it was Anna returning, ready to pick up where they'd left off only moments ago. He turned to see Pamina enter the room, a look of reproach on her face.

"Abra, what are you up to now?" She clicked her tongue at the fat cat circling Daniel's leg. He looked down at the ball of black weaving in and out of his legs. When the heck had Abra entered the room? He was pretty damn stealthy for an overweight tomcat.

Abra made a weird sound and jumped into Pamina's arms. Once nestled in the crook of her elbow he purred loudly and dragged his paw over one breast. Pamina tapped him on the nose and gave him an admonishing glare. "I don't think so."

Half-amused and half-disturbed at the bizarre encounter, Daniel wondered what kind of silent exchange was taking place between them. Then again, perhaps he was better off not knowing. Abra made another loud purring sound, and amusement danced in Pamina's eyes as she laughed and gently tossed him out the door. Miffed, Abra offered her his backside and sauntered into another room.

Pamina turned her attention to him and presented a professional face. "Did Anna lay out the details to you and go over her designs?"

He laid the sketchpad down and drove his hands into his pockets. "Yes, I'm all set."

Padding softly, Pamina circled the room and ran her hand along the down bedding. Her mystical green eyes glistened. "Odd, isn't it?"

"Odd?"

"Yes, that a woman who no longer believes in romance and happily-ever-after is designing a room for just such a thing. Almost as if deep down in some secret compartment, she still holds a modicum of hope that she's wrong."

Apprehension surged inside him. Daniel's mind raced, recalling her statement about romance and Prince Charming, and how she no longer believed it was in the cards for her. Why would she think such a thing?

A well-used paperback seemed to materialize on the

nightstand. He hadn't noticed it when he'd first catalogued the room. Pamina picked it up and thumbed through the pages. Daniel recognized the book as Anna's. He'd seen her with dozens of similar novels over the years, all well loved and dog-eared. What was in those passages that had her wanting to reread them?

"But since she's sworn off men and relationships, I guess she'll never find out if true love really does exist."

Unease moved through him and cooled his blood. "Why would she swear off men?" Had someone hurt her? So help him, if anyone had dared hurt the woman he was crazy about, they'd have hell to pay.

His brothers had kept tabs on her over the years. They'd seen many men come in and out of her life, the same way women had come in and out of his. It appeared that neither one of them was able to commit to anything for any length of time, as if she was holding out for him the way he was holding out for her. Wishful thinking, he knew, especially considering she kept pushing him away.

"Something happened, a long time ago, and it caused her to cool on the opposite sex."

His searched his memories. Was it around the same time she'd cooled on him?

Pamina put the book down, reached into her pocket, pulled out a crisp red apple and took a generous bite. An odd tingling trickled through his bloodstream as she sailed past him. She gave him a peculiar look, tapped him on the shoulder, and around a mouthful of apple said, "I'll leave you to it, Daniel. I believe you have a lot of work to do."

Why did he get the sneaking suspicion that she wasn't talking about the work she'd hired him to do? Nevertheless, after she left he made his way across the room and grabbed the book. He turned it over in his hand and read the back cover. Then he flipped the pages open that had been dog-eared, and read the passages.

Okay, now that he hadn't anticipated. Maybe Anna was onto something here. No wonder she was hooked.

Twenty minutes later, after speed-reading his way through half the book, he sank down on the bed and wiped his brow. As he considered the hero in the story, he could only assume it was the kind of guy Anna wanted. Strong, confident, a take-charge kind of guy. Not at all like the bumbling idiot she'd always reduced him to. He really hadn't expected to be so nervous around her. He chewed on that a moment longer. After reading all these novels, perhaps Anna felt romance wasn't in the cards because no man could live up to her expectation. He certainly wasn't behaving like a romance novel hero with the edgy, juvenile way he was acting, all nervous and shaky when she was close. He tapped the book against his palm and made a decision. If this was the kind of guy she wanted, this was the kind of guy he was going to give her. But first, more research was in order.

Chapter Three

As the scent of freshly baked apple and cinnamon muffins filled the air, Anna snapped her cell phone shut and pursed her lips in thought as she leaned against the bottom post of the long winding staircase. She'd spent the last couple of days wondering when her mother was going to call to let her know that Daniel was back in town. Now she knew. Honestly, her mother, a romantic like Anna, was still holding out hope that the two of them would eventually get together. She certainly wasn't going to burst her mother's bubble and tell her Daniel wasn't the sweet "boy next door" she thought he was.

Her mom had called to invite her to a dinner party that night, insisting she must attend because she hadn't been by in weeks, but once Anna found out that she'd also invited Daniel and his family she flat-out refused. Working in confined quarters with him for the last couple of days had been hard enough. Seeing him all hot, sweaty, sexy, and sporting a tool belt, no less, while he worked with those deft hands of his, had played havoc with her libido. So much so that she'd actually worn down the batteries on her favorite vibrator. Sadly, her little rabbit would hop no more. She couldn't imagine what it'd do to her to see Daniel all cleaned up. And boy, oh boy, she could only imagine how well Daniel, the man, would clean up.

"Everything okay?"

The deep, raspy sound of his voice sent shivers skittering through her. Of course everything wasn't okay. How could they be okay, not when every time she turned around, the man she was crazy about—still crazy about dammit, despite the heartache he'd put her though—was looming over her, looking like sex incarnate, and blatantly turning on the charm. Was he determined to finally do her in, or better yet, melt her resolve and get her into his bed?

Heck, maybe she should just do it. Maybe that would get him out of her system once and for all. Oh hell! Who was she kidding? One night in his bed would be emotional suicide at best. There'd be no coming back from that.

Working to keep her emotions under wraps, she turned to him at the same time he stepped closer. Their bodies collided and he wrapped his hand around her waist to anchor her to him. Anna swallowed, fabricated a smile and extricated herself from his tenuous hold. Gathering her composure, she shook the phone.

"My mom. She invited me to dinner."

He angled his head and his warm cinnamon-scented breath washed over her cheeks. "Are you going?"

"No. I'm working late tonight." The truth was, she'd been waiting for Daniel to leave so she could have the room to herself. Then she could finally install the curtains and arrange the pillows, accessories and furniture, without the distraction of his hard body hindering her attention.

"I'm working late too."

"Oh." Well then, that changed everything. If Daniel was going to be here, she certainly wasn't. But he didn't need to know that, otherwise he might change his plans.

His glance dropped to her chest, making her feel very self-conscious. She pressed harder against the banister, the post indenting her back. At first she thought he was ogling her cleavage, slightly exposed in her V-neck T-shirt. But then something in his eyes softened, and beneath the surface she could see sadness.

"What?" she asked.

"Your necklace."

Anna slipped her fingers under the chain and gently ran the soft pad of her thumb along the gold. "What about it?"

He rolled one shoulder. "Nothing really. I just remember how happy you were when your mother gave it to you."

"During my sweet-sixteen party," she said absently, as she recalled that evening so long ago. It was the only nice thing about that night. She'd tried to put on a good show for her guests, playing the happy party girl, but deep inside she was miserable and dejected because the one guy she wanted to be dancing with under the stars wasn't there.

Another thought struck. How did he know about the necklace? Had he been spying on her that night too?

A perplexed frown crossed his face. "About that night..."

Dammit, she didn't want to dredge up those painful memories again. Not now. Not here. And definitely not with him. Before she had a chance to respond, his cell phone rang and he excused himself.

Anna swallowed her unease and turned her focus to the ironing board and sewing machine she'd set up in the front room, and to the curtains awaiting her attention. She sat down, prepared to run the hem through the serger when Candace showed up, looking a little hot, bothered and flustered herself. Anna wasn't surprised, really. She'd seen the man Pamina had hired to help Candace build furniture. She wondered if her friend was having as hard a time as she was at keeping to the pact.

188

"Lunch?" Candace asked.

Anna powered down the serger, deciding a few minutes away from the inn was exactly what she needed.

"Love to," she said eagerly. "Let's check in with Lindsay." Perhaps over lunch they could all reaffirm their vow to steer clear of men and that would help get her head on straight and her focus back on her work, where it belonged.

Anna and Candace climbed the staircase and popped into Lindsay's room, which was coming along quite nicely. Unfortunately Lindsay couldn't join them because her shipment of BDSM equipment had just arrived. Too bad. With the way Daniel was affecting her, Anna really could have used a good stern talking to.

A few minutes later they stepped out into the fresh outdoors and walked down the street to the quaint restaurant around the corner. After lunch, Candace decided to go for a run, while Anna returned to her curtains. Much to her delight, the rest of the day passed quickly, with no incidents or encounters with Daniel. He stayed in the room working, and she stayed on the main level sewing and ironing.

As nighttime closed around them, Anna tidied her work area, checked in with her partners, then headed back to her condo. Her mother was right. She'd been so busy working that she hadn't had time to visit. So tonight, with Daniel tied up in the room, it seemed like the perfect night to attend their dinner party and placate them.

Less than an hour later, dressed in her comfy jeans and a knit sweater, she exited her condo and jumped into her car. Her breath turned to fog as she turned her engine over and flicked on the heater. Even though the days were warm and sunny, the nights had turned cool and brisk, a sure sign winter was just around the corner.

The streets were fairly quiet as she made her way to her parents. Numerous cars lined the driveway as well as the cul-de-sac, and Anna smiled, thinking this was just the thing to take her mind off matters for a while.

With her mom and dad's driveway full, she parked on the street, just outside Daniel's parents' house, and made her way up the walkway to the home that she'd grown up in. Her designer's eye took in the beautifully finished two-story with its welcoming country decor. Her mother really did have a knack. Anna had obviously come by her designer skills honestly. Laughter and music reached her ears as she pushed open the front door. Her mother, Margaret, moved through the crowd to greet her, a wide smile on her pretty face.

"I'm so glad you decided to come." She looked past Anna's shoulders. Her mother frowned as she tucked a silver strand of hair behind her ear, a habit Anna had picked up long ago. "Is Daniel with you?"

"Why would Daniel be with me?"

"Well he's working with you, isn't he?"

"That doesn't mean we travel together. Besides, he's working late." Her mother's eyes sparkled, like she knew something Anna didn't. Needing to set her straight, Anna cupped her mother's hand. "Mom, look. Daniel and I are just friends. Nothing will ever develop between us."

"We'll see."

Anna rolled her eyes heavenward and groaned, "Mom," but she knew any efforts to convince her mother otherwise were futile. Simply and utterly futile. When her mother put her mind to something, there was no changing it.

Ignoring her protest, her mother ushered her to the dining room, and with a wave of her hand she gestured for the other guests to follow. Anna gave her father a kiss on the cheek and took her regular seat. She politely smiled at Daniel's parents, who sat across from her and were assessing her over the brims of their wine glasses. Then she proceeded to exchange pleasantries with the three other couples who gathered around the long oaken table, which was dressed in a vibrant orange and red tablecloth, perfect autumn colors. Anna was quick to notice that the seat beside her was still empty, and she could only guess who it was meant for.

Anna inhaled and took in the medley of food in the center of the table. Her stomach grumbled. Goodness, she'd forgotten how much she loved her mother's home cooking. As everyone began to fill their plates and Anna helped herself to a heaping spoonful of mashed potato, her mother initiated conversation.

"So, Anna, I haven't seen you in a while. Is there anyone special in your life that you'd like to tell us about?"

With the serving spoon poised over her plate, Anna was about to open her mouth and tell her mother no, but slammed it again when questions about her marital status—or lack thereof—came at her fast and hard from the other women sitting around the table.

"Are you dating anyone?"

"Do you have any plans to get married?"

"Have you met Mr. Right yet?"

"Have you and Daniel gone out yet?"

"He's back for good now, you know."

"Time for that boy to settle down too."

Okay, this was a twist she hadn't—yet should have—expected from her parents' longtime friends. She loved her mother, she really did, and understood she only wanted what was best for Anna, but this was too much. She glanced at her father who simply offered her an apologetic look. Feeling like she had just been put before the firing squad, Anna blinked, dropped the scoop of potato onto her plate and tried to keep up with the next round of questions.

As her appetite dissolved and she remained tight lipped, the guests began to talk amongst themselves, speculating on Daniel's sudden return home, and it became clear to Anna that everyone in the room thought she and Daniel belonged together. After a moment of reprieve from their questions, they turned their attention back to her.

Anna glared at her mother, but Margaret presented her with a polite smile in response. She worked to keep her temper in check as she removed her napkin from her lap. She was just about to toss it onto the table and set the record straight, when a voice in the doorway stopped her cold.

"Why don't we let Anna eat and save the questions for later? The poor girl has been working day and night and is in need of nourishment. Look at her, she's dwindling away to nothing." His tone was soft and easy, but commanding nonetheless. Beneath that humor, Daniel meant business, and for that she was grateful.

He stood in the archway, his large body practically blocking the light from the other room. With body-molding jeans riding low on his hips, and a black leather jacket that accentuated his broad shoulder and fit body, the man looked like sin and seduction all rolled into one delectable package. Dammit, did he have to clean up that nicely? As she stared at him and took pleasure in his attire, it occurred to her that like some real-life Prince Charming, Daniel had come to her rescue.

The incessant chatter around the room stopped as all eyes turned to Daniel. With a sexy half-grin on his mouth, he removed his coat to showcase a gorgeous chest and tight abs emphasized beneath his button-down dress shirt. He crossed the room, dropped a kiss onto his mother's cheek then took his seat beside Anna. After a round of greetings, Daniel effortlessly redirected conversation and in no time at all, everyone went back to filling their plates.

Anna turned to Daniel and spoke in a low voice as they exchanged a long, heated look. "I thought you said you had work to do."

He arched a brow. "I could say the same about you."

Okay, so he had a point there.

"Changed my mind. A girl has a right to do that you know."

He grinned, and shot back, "And what, a guy doesn't? Hey what's good for the goose."

"So I'm a goose now, am I? And a scrawny one at that, apparently." She feigned insult, but Daniel's soft laugh soon had her smiling.

His grin broadened. "Would you have preferred I'd let them go on?"

"I supposed you're looking for a thank-you?"

He angled his head. "A thank-you would be nice." Something about the way he said that had desire skittering through her veins.

"Fine then..."

He held his hand up to stop her. "Wait. You can thank me later."

She pursed her lips, wondering what he was up to, but he simply gave her a devilish look and turned the conversation to his progress on the guestroom, entering into safe, common ground, she supposed.

They spent the next thirty minutes talking about the room and her ideas. He listened with interest and for a moment there, it felt like old times when they'd chat about nothing and everything over the backyard fence. Once the dishes were cleared, the guests made their way to the other room for after dinner drinks, and Daniel went to speak to his parents.

As everyone mingled, Anna tried to blend into the background, but from across the room Daniel spotted her inching toward the door. When his eyes locked on hers and a predatory smile crossed his face, he sidestepped the other guests to close the gap between them.

Anna swallowed and tucked her hair behind her ear. Oh God, how she wanted him. As warmth moved through her, she began to question the logic behind the pact and the logic behind denying her needs.

He eased in beside her and arched a brow. "Looking for a quick getaway?"

Anna smirked. "That obvious?"

"To me it is."

"Oh really? Aren't you astute?"

"I just know you, Anna."

"You don't know me, Daniel. I'm not that same naïve girl I was back in high school."

Two drinks in hand, her mother stepped up beside them, a glint in her blue eyes. "It's nice to see you two getting reacquainted." She held the drinks out, but neither one accepted.

Daniel cleared his throat. "I was just trying to convince Anna here to take in a football game with me."

Anna's head came back with a start and she swatted him in the stomach, only to meet with a wall of muscles. "What? You were not."

"Oh, Anna, that's a great idea. Come by tomorrow and we can pack a picnic basket. I just picked up some fresh bread and cheese, and I just bought these great wine glasses..." As her mother droned on, Anna gave a slow shake of her head. So much for Prince Charming coming to the rescue. Daniel stood over her, looking all innocent and sweet as he rocked back and forth on his heels. But Anna knew him for what he really was, the devil in disguise.

No longer in the mood to make conversation, Anna excused herself and stepped outside for some fresh air. With everyone mingling, she suspected her temporary absence wouldn't be noticed, and after a refueling breath, she would step back inside, give her goodbyes then make her way home. As she strolled around the garden, to the spot where she used to indulge in one of her romance novels or play with room designs, her glance went to Daniel's bedroom window and to the tall, towering maple tree that she'd seen him climb down a time or two, when he used to sneak out at night. Okay, okay so maybe he hadn't been the only one doing the spying.

She gave a heavy sigh. The truth was, she'd wanted to be the girl he was sneaking out to see, or better yet, the girl he was sneaking in to his bedroom. It had been something she'd fantasized about for years.

The wind picked up, and as she hugged herself to stave off a shiver, heavy footsteps heralded someone's approach. She turned around and came face to face with Daniel. The second his body came into contact with hers and she caught a whiff of his warm, familiar scent, heat unfurled inside her, and she struggled to maintain a coherent thought.

"You cold?" He pulled her close and ran his hands up and down her arms, but the friction merely created heat in the needy spot between her legs.

"I'm okay."

Daniel slipped off his jacket, draped it over her shoulders, and pulled her in tight. Feeling warm and wanting and in need of a distraction, she glanced at the towering maple tree. She momentarily wondered if his parents had redesigned his room after he'd left, or if they'd left it the way it was. Not that she knew how it was before his departure, since he'd never invited her in.

"Want to climb it?"

She chuckled as her body absorbed his warmth. "I don't think so."

He gave her a boyish wink. "Come on, it'll be fun."

"Fun?"

"Where's your adventurous side, Anna?"

"I'm not dressed for climbing trees." Her voice lacked conviction.

"It's your only way out, you know." He pulled a face, fear dancing in his eyes as he pointed to her parents' living room. "Unless you want to go back in there with those sharks, you don't have a choice." He gave a mock shiver. "I've never seen such an interrogation. When I first arrived I thought I was in the middle of an intervention."

Anna laughed and Daniel joined in, and in that instant, she felt like the world had been lifted from her shoulders. Honestly, she'd been strung so tight over the last few days it felt so good to laugh, to let go for a few minutes.

"It's *was* an intervention," she said. "A let's-get-Anna-hitched sneak attack." She paused to shake her head. "I didn't see it coming."

He touched her gold chain, and when his warm fingers grazed her skin, her hands curled in his shirt. Eyes smoldering, he wet his mouth and in a low voice said, "I think they only have your best interests at heart."

Needing to lighten things up before she went to mush in his arms and remembering how he'd toyed with her mother, she whacked him on the shoulder and he let loose a moan.

"Hey, what's with all the abuse?" he questioned, faking exasperation. But that exasperation quickly gave way to passion. "You keep it up and you're going to get a spanking of your own."

Anna's breath grew shallow, and she gulped air, trying for normal. "What's with teasing my mother like that and telling her you wanted me to go to a football game? She'll be clinging to that for weeks. You know as well as I do that she wants us together."

Without an ounce of humor in his voice, he said, "So do I, Anna."

Her insides twisted. Okay, she understood he wanted her physically, the last few days had proven that. But what she wasn't sure about was why. Because she was the one he couldn't have? Or had he changed and matured over the years, and like her, knew how good they could have been together?

"Why, Daniel. Why do you want this?"

He ran his thumb over her bottom lip. Despite the cold, her cheeks flushed hot and her legs felt a little shaky beneath her. The tender intimate way he looked at her took her breath away. Heaven help her, she was fighting a losing battle here. He was charming, seductive, persuasive—the attraction far too powerful for her to ignore any longer. "Daniel—"

Instead of answering her, he grabbed her hand and tugged. "Come on."

"Where?"

He gestured toward the huge tree branch that hung over the fence. "We're going up. I'll show you the view."

With unhurried movements, he dropped her hand and grabbed the branch to test it. As he pulled himself up, her glance moved to his perfect backside, enjoying the view from where she stood. Instantly, with her brain on overdrive, she couldn't help but think that maybe, just maybe he was right and an adventure was in order. And she wasn't necessarily talking about climbing the tree.

As she warmed to the idea, she slipped her arms through his coat, zippered it, then grabbed the branch to climb. Her tight jeans protested the movement. "These are my favorite jeans, so help me if I rip them—"

"I'll buy you a new pair," he offered and reached down a helping hand.

She scoffed, half-heartedly, aware that she found the situation a little exciting. Not to mention fun and spontaneous. "Couldn't we be normal adults and use the front door? I'm not really a fan of heights."

"Nope. The only way to my front door, is through your front door. And since you're avoiding the sharks..."

He was right, the fence circled the yards, and she wasn't quite ready to go inside and face another swarming.

"Plus this is a little exciting, don't you think?" he teased with a wink. "Sneaking into my room late at night."

In spite of herself she laughed. "I've had more excitement watching paint dry," she lied, masking her enthusiasm. Heck, she didn't want to make this too easy on him, letting him think he was finally going to get what he'd been after for years.

But deep inside her she was excited. Damn excited. Growing up, Anna had always been a rule follower and had never done anything quite like this before. Being here with Daniel and climbing this tree took her back to her teen years when she used to go to bed and dream about sneaking into his room with him, dream about being the one girl he wanted, really wanted.

She grabbed his hand and he hauled her higher. Once they reached the top, Daniel shimmied his window open, climbed inside, then helped her in.

When her flats hit the floor, she let out a breath. Feeling much more comfortable on solid footing, she shut the window behind her. Daniel flicked on his lamp, and as the warm light bathed the room, she took in the décor. A single bed was up against one wall, a navy blue comforter haphazardly thrown over it. On the other wall, there was an open laptop sitting on a small wooden student desk. Trophies and medals adorned the numerous shelves above the bed, and a football lamp sat on his nightstand.

"Nice room."

He walked across the floor and locked his door. A fine tingle ran through her. Despite being all grown up, something about sneaking into his room felt so forbidden, and it shocked her how much that excited her.

"It's a shrine," he teased. "Mom left it the way it was, hoping I'd come back to it I guess."

"Now her wish has come true. You're staying here, aren't you?"

He grinned. "Just temporarily." Something strange passed over his eyes—it was the same look he'd given her earlier but one she didn't recognize—when he went on to announce, "I bought the old Murphy house down by the lake. Now I'm just waiting for my goods to arrive. I never thought they'd sell it, but lucky for me, the Murphys recently retired and moved to Florida."

"You bought the old Murphy place?" She widened her eyes in surprise. "I love that place."

Again, there was that odd look. "I know you do."

She pulled a face. "You suddenly seem to know an awful lot."

He backed her up until her knees hit the bed, and something in his voice hitched. "I know a lot more about you than you think I do."

Her heart raced, her body grew damp and needy, and her voice came out a little rough around the edges. "And I think you're a sweet talker."

He offered her a cocky grin, and she damn near wilted. "Is it working?"

"No."

"Then why are your cheeks flushed?"

As his primal essence completely overwhelmed her, she responded, "Because it was cold out."

"And your body, it's trembling."

"Like I said, it's cold outside."

In a move that took her by surprise, he pulled her close, anchoring her body to his and she could feel his arousal press against her midriff. His cock felt glorious, hard and primed to go, and it took all her willpower not to moan out loud and rub up against it. As her body burned with desire and pent-up passion, pleasure gathered between her legs. She placed her hands on his shoulders, and in a bold move that seemed to catch him off guard, she ran her fingers over his muscles and could feel strength radiating off him.

Daniel swallowed and his powerful hands shook like a juvenile on his first date as they slipped around her back. "And...what about...your nipples...?" His words came out a broken, choppy. "Are they hard because it's cold out too?"

His cock pressed against her stomach. "I could be asking

you the same question."

"Is it my nipples you're talking about, Anna? Or something else?" he teased, his voice a little rusty as he gave her a boyish grin that turned her inside out.

As she enjoyed the sexy banter, he dipped his head, the light from the lamp washing over his face and making him look so sweet and innocent. Angelic, even. When she parted her lips, he drew a deep, sharp breath. "Do you have any idea how long I've wanted to kiss you?"

She gave a needy sigh. "What are you waiting for?"

The muscles along his jaw tightened, and with the way his heart was crashing against his chest, she feared he might black out. He gave a tortured moan and stuttered when he tried to explain. "I don't know. I guess I just want to get this right." His confession immediately brought them to a deeper level of intimacy and everything inside her reached out to him.

Anna laughed lightly, sensing a new closeness between them. Clearly it was difficult to have divulged something that private. He brushed his thumb over her bottom lip, and seeing him flustered by their proximity bolstered her confidence. "No worries, Daniel. I have a feeling you're going to get it right."

His body quivered, and his gaze was dark, turbulent. His breath came in a low rush. "And if I don't?"

Good God, he was nervous. Not only was it was written all over his face, it was in his body language and in his voice when he spoke. That same nervousness had always gotten to her, touched her deep and turned her to mush. But was it a ploy or was he sincere? Surely no man could fake distress like that.

The look on his face was so intense, it was both exhilarating and frightening and prompted her into action. She, in turn, gave him a look that conveyed her needs, still hardly able to believe she was here with him.

"Kiss me, Daniel," she begged, her voice low and sultry. As desire clouded her thoughts, she opened herself up to him, giving herself to him the way she'd sworn she'd never do.

With that his lips closed over hers. At first touch her world tilted on its axis, making her feel heady and dizzy. His tongue moved into her mouth and tangled with hers, tasting, touching, teasing her, and fuelling her lust.

His kiss was deep and sensual, and had her aching to the core. She closed her eyes and pulled his tongue in deeper. As she pressed against him, he groaned and she writhed like a wanton woman in response, unable to assuage the need exploding inside her. From head to toe, her skin grew hot, and she was pretty certain if he didn't soon throw her on that bed and take her—hard, deep and long—she'd go up in a burst of flames.

His hands slid over her body, shaping and palming her curves and leaving fire in their wake. As he pillaged her mouth with hunger and touched her intimately, she frantically tore at his shirt, not wanting to wait one more second to feel his naked skin on hers.

Daniel slipped his hands under the coat she still wore, and ran his fingers over her flesh. Little bumps of pleasure broke out on her skin. His scent enveloped her, and she inhaled deeply, pulling it into her lungs. Bloody hell she wanted him. And she was determined to finally have him, no matter what tomorrow brought.

He slipped his coat off her shoulders and let it fall to the floor. Just as he moved to pull her sweater over her head, a noise downstairs drew their attention and stopped them cold.

"Daniel, are you up there?" his mother asked.

"Oh fuck," he murmured and pressed his lips to her forehead, his breathing labored and heavy.

Anna gripped him for support and rested her chin against his chest, as she tried to tamp down her lust.

"My parents," he whispered, stating the obvious.

She nodded. "Party must be over."

He shook his head. "Christ, I can't wait until we take possession of our own place."

Flustered, and barely able to understand his words, Anna inched back. His mind must be as lust-crazed as hers. Because surely he meant to say when *he* took possession of *his* own place. As she stood before him, all hot and bothered, and in desperate need of release she said nervously, "I should go." She glanced at the window, her escape route. "I don't want to be caught in here with you. It might give everyone the wrong idea."

"Or the right idea," he offered, stepping into her until their bodies collided.

Her brain was so passion rattled she didn't even know what he meant by that. Did he want just one night of sex with her, or did he want more? Did she even dare hope for the latter? "Daniel—"

He cut her off and pointed to his window. "Okay, you go that way so no one sees you, and I'll go downstairs to distract my parents."

She nodded and appreciated that he respected her need for privacy. But she hated that this night had come to an end so abruptly. She'd spent numerous years fantasizing about this man and this moment, and just when she was about to experience the pleasure of his lovemaking, once and for all, forgetting about past hurts or even what the morning brought, their night had come to a grinding halt. Perhaps some things just weren't meant to be.

She turned her back to him. "I'll see you later then." She tried to keep the disappointment from her voice but failed miserably.

He grabbed her, spun her around and meshed her groin to his. "You're not getting off the hook that easily."

"What do you mean?"

His grin turned wicked. "You still owe me."

"Owe you?"

"A thank-you, remember."

"Oh right. Th—"

He pressed his fingers to her lips to hush her. "You can thank me by coming back to the inn with me. I've been working hard and want to show you what I've accomplished."

"I don't think tonight..." Even though she was anxious to see his handiwork, as he'd been banging around in that room alone all day, she just needed to get home, jump into a cold shower and pull herself together.

His gaze slid over her and bombarded her with desire. "You have to come tonight," he commanded in a soft voice, one that told her he had no intention of taking no for an answer.

As her skin flushed hotly, she inched backwards and moved toward the window. Each step brought her closer to his desk, and that's when she noticed the stack of books behind his laptop. What the heck? Since when had Daniel started reading romance novels? She was about to ask, but he stepped in front of the pile, as if to block her line of sight, and in a firm tone, said, "Tonight, Anna."

He had an odd look on his face and there was an urgency in his voice that she hadn't heard before. She paused, wondering exactly what it was that he *really* wanted to show her. Was it the room, or was it something else entirely?

She gave a resigned sigh. "Okay, but just for a few minutes." She opened the window, stuck her foot out, and shot one last glance his way. "By the way," she murmured quietly. "The kiss was perfect, Daniel. Just like I knew it would be."

Something about the genuine smile he sent her way had an invisible band tightening around her heart, and she knew she was in serious trouble here, because any more time spent with him would draw her in so deep, not even a compass could help her find her way out.

Chapter Four

Daniel hurried to the inn, desperate to get there before Anna so he could make the final arrangements and address any deficiencies in the room. Since she had to go through her parents' house first and would undoubtedly face another inquisition, he had plenty of time to set the stage for a night of sweet seduction.

He pulled his van into the driveway, killed the ignition and rushed toward the inn. He shot a glance around and spotted two other vehicles nearby. All was quiet in the neighborhood, and as he navigated the walkway, he took note of Candace and Lindsay's respective rooms. From his ground-level view he could see the lights were still on, and he wondered if they were all working late. Or maybe something else was going on up there. He'd seen the sideways glances between Anna's colleagues and the men Pamina had hired to help them. Not to mention the array of sex equipment set up in their rooms, just begging to be tested.

Daniel climbed the stairs and met with Abra on the top landing. As Abra's impenetrable, almond-shaped eyes gave him a once-over, they seemed to glisten with ancient knowledge and universal wisdom. It occurred to Daniel that it was the same peculiar look he'd seen the mystical Pamina give the girls a time or two. As he studied the cat, he had the sneaking suspicion that beneath that ball of fur, Abra was more than just a mere feline. Daniel shook his head and scoffed, brushing off that crazy thought.

But seriously, if he didn't know better, he'd think there was some magical force bringing the couples together at the inn, and Pamina, along with her cat, was somehow behind it all.

Not wanting to disturb the other members of the household, he quietly opened the door and stepped inside. As he shut it, he noticed the way his hands had begun to shake. Jesus, he couldn't believe how nervous he felt.

Nerves, however, played no part in tonight's seduction. After reading all those romance novels, it was glaringly apparent what kind of man Anna liked and what kind she didn't. Right now, with his knees knocking and his heart pounding, he definitely fit into the latter.

Gathering himself, he drove his hands into his pockets and bolted upstairs. Once inside the room, he lit the candles, started a fire in the newly designed fireplace and then stepped back to take in the ambiance. He'd spent hours preparing the room to make it just right for Anna—a woman like Anna deserved nothing but the best—and he prayed she'd be pleased with his efforts. Once he was personally satisfied with the setting, he opened a bottle of wine to let it breathe, before making his way downstairs to gather the rest of the supplies.

Five minutes later he stood waiting at the foot of the stairs, trying to quiet his pounding heart. The shoes tapping a steady beat on the walkway outside heralded Anna's approach. He drew a calming breath as Anna climbed the steps and pushed open the front door. The sight of her perfect body, silhouetted by the golden streetlights, made him quake in anticipation. She was about to flick on the switch when he stepped forward and put his hand over hers to stop her. He wanted her all to himself and was not about to draw unnecessary attention to them.

"Hi, Anna."

"Hi," she murmured, sounding breathless and looking a little startled to see him waiting for her. "You got here fast."

He put his mouth closer to hers and whispered, "That's because I didn't want to waste a minute." He pressed against her and could feel heat rising in her body.

"You...uh...you wanted to show me something?"

He gathered her hand in his and led her to the staircase. "I think everyone is still working. We should be quiet so we don't disturb them."

"Okay." She lowered her voice to match his. "They're probably staying overnight. Sometimes when we're on a deadline, we don't like to waste time traveling."

He arched a curious brow. "So no one would think it odd if you stayed overnight?"

"No, not at all. Why?" Anna tucked a strand of hair behind her ear, and blinked up at him.

"No reason." None that he wanted to share right now, anyway. If things went according to plan, neither one of them would be going anywhere tonight. But if she got caught with him in the morning, he didn't want her to feel uncomfortable. She was a private person, and he respected that.

Padding softly they climbed the stairs, and Daniel led her down the hall, anxious to pick up where they'd left off at his place. He pushed open the door, and ushered her inside. When Anna gasped and put her hand on her chest, he couldn't help but smile, pleasure welling up inside him.

"Daniel, it's beautiful," she said, her eyes wide in surprise as she took in the room and drew a breath to pull in the aroma from jasmine-scented candles. "So elegant and romantic." She turned to see the fireplace, now fully restored and brandishing a blazing fire. "You've been busy."

She stepped farther into the room and stopped abruptly when she noticed the small round table set for two, a bottle of wine chilling in a bucket of ice water, and a fruit and cheese tray in the center of the table.

"So I take it this is what you wanted to show me?"

He laughed lightly, but it sounded edgy, even to him. He tried to tamp down his nerves as he stepped up behind her. He pressed her against his chest, and his cock brushed along the small of her back.

"Well, yes. Among other things," he murmured.

"I see…"

And see she did, because the tremble in her body told him she knew exactly what he was referring to.

He turned her in his arms. "You said you wanted to design a room that inspired romance. So I figured we should try it ourselves first. If it can't inspire romance and seduction for us, then it's not going to inspire it for others, right?"

"So, this is all about research then?"

"I take my job seriously, Anna. And I like to leave my clients very, very satisfied."

He listened to her throat as she swallowed. "Leaving a client satisfied is pretty essential in a small town." His gaze fixed on her lips as she wet them with the soft blade of her tongue. "Where word of mouth is most crucial."

Speaking of mouths…

"Most crucial indeed." Daniel slid his hand down her back, enjoying the feel of her curves, and guided her to the table. He pulled out the chair and gestured with a nod. "Have a seat."

As she obliged, he walked over to the radio and turned on

the music. A soft romantic tune filled the air as embers sparked in the fireplace, drifting upward and creating warm shadows over Anna's face.

She smiled up at him. "Everything looks gorgeous."

"Yes, everything does," he said sincerely as they exchanged a long lingering look.

She toyed with the stem of the wine glass and glanced past his shoulder at the fire. "I never knew you were so romantic."

He sat, poured two glasses of wine and grabbed a strawberry from the platter. "There are a lot of things you don't know about me, and I think we should rectify that. Starting now."

She took a sip of her wine and he poised the strawberry over her mouth. "Open."

When she parted her lips, he squeezed the berry, letting the juice run over her lips and down her chin. Her pretty pink tongue darted out to lap at the juice, but he had a better idea. Daniel leaned across the table and brushed his mouth over her lips and chin. As the distinct taste of Anna, combined with the sweet strawberry flavor, exploded on his tongue, he damn near lost it then and there.

He moaned. "Mmmm..."

"Delicious," she agreed.

As firelight flickered over them, he watched color bloom high on her cheeks. She waved her hand in front of her face to cool herself down.

"Are you getting warm?" he asked.

She took another small sip of her wine then grabbed the hem of her sweater and waved it. "Downright hot," she said boldly, a playful gleam in her eyes. "You?"

Rattled, he swallowed a tortured moan, his muscles

tightening, his cock thickening, his body raging with lust. The passionate look on her face spoke of desire and need, and tonight he planned to give her exactly what she wanted. He just needed to keep it together. But Jesus, he'd wanted her for so long and needed her like he'd never needed another, that it was impossible to maintain his cool. As flames surged inside him and filled him with raw hunger, he shifted restlessly and tried for casual.

"I guess it's a...little warm in here," he responded.

When his voice came out choppy, something inside her seemed to give, and a tender look came over her face. "Daniel?" She leaned in and her mouth was so close he could feel her warm breath on his skin. Her hand touched his and her soft fingers scorched his flesh. "It's not just a little warm in here. It's hot, and you're burning up."

As though sensing his discomfort, she took the lead, climbed from her seat and closed the small gap between them. Seductive eyes met his as she stood at his side. He loved the way she moved, so easy and sexy. Not to mention the way his sweet, innocent Anna was taking charge. It totally blew his mind and excited the hell out of him.

When she touched his face, Daniel marveled at the change in her. He pushed his chair back to face her, and she threw one leg over his until she was straddling him. She writhed and centered her hot pussy over his aching cock.

Sweet fuck!

Deft fingers went to his buttons and the little vixen slowly undid them. "I know just how to cool you down."

His breath came in a low rush. "Oh yeah?"

She peeled his shirt off, then grabbed a strawberry from the tray. Holding it over his chest she squeezed it, letting the cool juice drip over his skin. He shivered in response.

"Feel better?" Her blue eyes darkened and were scalding with passion as she watched the nectar drip to his waistband.

"Not yet," he managed to get out.

She bent forward and her tongue singed his flesh as she followed the path to his jeans. His internal temperature skyrocketed, and it was all he could do to catch his breath. He gulped air and his mind began to swim with delicious ideas. Like how he wanted to peel her clothes away, lay her out on the rug in front of the fire and spend the night between her legs.

"How about now?" She ran her fingers over his chest. Her touch was erotic and intimate, and fuelled his lust.

As his blood boiled, his body shook all over and his words came out choppy. "Far from it, sweetheart." He ran shaky hands through her hair and shot her a smoldering look that conveyed his need.

"You're still hot?" Her voice was low, sultry, and everything in the way she was looking at him touched him on a deeper level. Fuck, he wanted her. Tonight. Tomorrow. Forever.

"Yeah, still hot."

She paused for a moment, then grinned at him. The sexy curve of her mouth filled him with passion and possessiveness.

"What?" he asked, not understanding the odd expression that had come over her.

Emotions played across her face. "I love it when you look at me like that." She brushed her finger over his lip and her touch seeped under his skin.

"Like what?" He pinched his eyes shut for a brief second and struggled to maintain control, but need stole every ounce of his strength.

Instead of answering she perused the room and murmured, "The ambiance really does inspire romance and seduction. You were right, a woman doesn't stand a chance." She laughed softly. "You've really outdone yourself."

"You deserve more."

She turned back to him quickly and dark lashes blinked over passion-imbued eyes. "Daniel..."

The way she said his name, so whispery soft, shattered any semblance of control he had left. Sudden, urgent need overcame him, and he was no longer able to fight down his carnal cravings. He wrapped his hands around her waist, anchoring her body to his, and stood up quickly.

"Whoa." She wrapped her arms around his neck to hold on. She'd better hold on tight because he was hell-bent on giving her the ride of her life. He pressed his mouth to hers and kissed her deeply as he carried her to the fire. The warmth from the flames moistened their skin and melded their bodies together.

Heat arced between them, and he forced himself to breathe slowly as he lowered her to her feet. Emotions pressed against his chest and he cleared his throat in an effort to summon a modicum of control. Anna wasn't like the others, and being with her was different. She was important to him, and he didn't want to screw it up.

When her soft hands touched his bare chest with purpose, he inched back and took a second to regroup.

"Are you okay?" There was genuine concern in her voice.

Shit. So much for acting like one of her romance-novel heroes. "Anna, I'm sorry," he confessed, feeling exasperated. "I don't know what's gotten into me. I'm not like this. Ever." He swayed back and forth and tried desperately to dispel his nervousness.

She stepped into him, her floral scent arousing him even more and throwing him off kilter. "But, Daniel, I like it."

He frowned, confused. "What? You do? Why?"

Her light chuckle curled around him as she gave him a look that suggested he was dense. "Don't you see, Daniel? That's what I've always liked about you."

With all his blood rushing south, he couldn't quite comprehend what she was telling him. He gathered her tight and felt her pert nipples against his bare chest. "I don't understand."

"What's not to understand? I love it when you show this side of yourself to me. I've never seen you do that with anyone else. No one can fake nervousness like that."

He wasn't exactly sure what she was talking about. Why would she think he was faking? He gave a quick shake of his passion-rattled brain and tried to make sense of things. "But the books you read. I thought you liked your men alpha, strong and take-charge."

She laughed. "You are all those things, Daniel. But you're more than that. You're kind and sensitive, and when you show me that side of yourself"—she pressed her hand over her heart—"it really gets to me."

"So you like bumbling idiots. Well that would have been nice to know before I spent all those hours on research."

Her jaw gaped open. "Is that what the romance novels are about? You were trying to become the man you thought I wanted."

His grin was sheepish. "Well..."

She whacked him playfully. "You really have changed, haven't you?"

Feeling much more at ease, he grabbed her hand and anchored it to her side. "Hey, what did I tell you about whacking me?"

"I...I don't remember." She nibbled her bottom lip in a good show of innocence.

Well, I'll be damned.

"So it seems you've changed too," he said.

"What do you mean?"

What he meant was that his sweet, romantic Anna wanted to be spanked. He let loose a laugh. There was more to this woman than he knew, and he was definitely going to enjoy every minute of getting to know her all over again.

He slid his hand down her back and gave her ass a good whack. Her lids flew open and her lips parted. As her eyes flared hot, her chest rose and fell rapidly, alerting him to her pleasure. "Oh my God!"

"You were warned." He drew his hand back for another whack. Jesus just the sight of her standing there, looking so aroused as he discovered her budding fantasies took his breath away. Desperately needing to see her naked, he grabbed the hem of her sweater and peeled it over her head, then made quick work of her pretty lace bra.

Shaky hands cupped her bare breasts and gave a light squeeze. When her beautiful rosy nipples poked out at him, he bent down and drew one into his mouth. Anna threw her head back and moaned. Christ, those sexy bedroom noises nearly pushed him over the edge.

Daniel slipped a hand between their bodies and worked the button on her jeans. The hiss of her zipper cut through the silence. She moved her hips restlessly as he peeled her pants off.

Then he stood back to look at her standing before the warm fire, desire—for him—written all over her face. In a sexy move, she hooked her thumb around the thin elastic on her panties and gave a little tug, offering him a glimpse of her smooth pubis.

As her gaze moved over his face, his lust mounted. "You forgot something," she said.

"No I didn't."

She arched a brow. "No."

"No, I left them for you to remove."

"Such a naughty boy. Maybe you're the one who needs to be spanked."

He grinned, loving this playful side of her. "Take your panties off, Anna."

With slow movements intended to entice, she inched her panties down, shimmying them ever so slowly. A smile lingered on her plump lips as her scent reached his nostrils. When she peeled away the scrap of material and tossed it on the rest of the pile, his breathing grew shallow.

Perspiration beaded on his forehead, his body aching to join with hers. "Now lie down on that rug and show me your pussy."

Anna sprawled on the fur mat before the fireplace, the moisture on her pussy glistening in the flames. She tilted her head and sexual energy leapt between them. Daniel swallowed and licked his lips.

When she reached for him, he quickly removed his clothes and climbed over her. She widened her legs to accommodate him and tangled her hands around his neck to draw him closer. Her body felt warm and silky beneath his, and all he could think about was burying himself in her and staying there for the rest of the night. Everything with her felt so intimate, so right.

His mouth found hers and he kissed her deeply, reveling in the things she made him feel. She moved her hips, brushing up against his shaft with her body, and he hardened to the point of pain. Fuck, he ached to be inside her but first he wanted to taste every inch of her skin. Beginning a downward path, he licked and tasted her sweet flesh. Nostrils flaring, he breathed in her scent then stopped to pull one of her nipples into his mouth. He sucked long and hard until her cries of pleasure filled the air.

His head came up with a start as a loud noise sounded from the room next door. Daniel smiled. "I guess these rooms aren't quite soundproof."

He flicked his tongue over her bellybutton, and she bit down on her bottom lip to suppress a cry. She spoke softly. "I guess we'd better keep it down before someone comes rushing in here to check on us."

Daniel shimmied lower and using his fingers, he parted her plump twin lips, then drew her feminine aroma deep into his lungs. He groaned low and deep. "I don't want you to keep it down, Anna. I love the sexy noises you make. Besides I think your friends are a little too busy to be concerned with what's going on in here." With that he brushed his thumb over her engorged clit and watched her hips come off the floor.

"Dear God!" she cried out, obviously no longer caring if anyone overheard her moans of pleasure.

"That's my girl," Daniel encouraged as he pushed a finger inside her tight opening. When he met with warm slick heat, he damned near lost his mind. "Baby, you're so wet."

"That's because I've been waiting for this for over a decade," she murmured.

With single-minded determination, she moved against his finger, her liquid silk burning his flesh and spurring him on. He dipped his head and made a slow pass with his tongue in an effort to draw out her pleasure. But he couldn't believe she was already there, hovering on the edge of release. Her cunt was pulsing and clenching around his probing index finger. He gave a slight wiggle of his finger, lightly brushing it over her G-spot. Moaning loudly, she went wild beneath him, her opening soaked his hand and instantly made him delirious with need.

"Jesus," he murmured as he lapped at her sweet cream, hardly able to believe how fast she'd orgasmed.

"It's been awhile," she confessed.

As he drank in her liquid silk, his cock ached and he pressed against her leg in desperate need of release. She gripped his shoulders and pulled him to her. Daniel climbed up her body and found her mouth. When she tasted her own sweetness on his lips, she moaned and he loved the sexy noises she made. In fact, he loved everything about her. Always had, and always will.

"I need you inside me," she whispered, her voice barely audible.

He groped for his pants, but when his search came up empty he asked, "Condom?"

Need crept into her voice when she rushed out, "I'm clean and I'm on the pill."

When she arched a questioning brow he assured her, "I am too."

Her eyes were bright with laugher, and her knowing grin, so slow and sweet, turned him inside out. "You're on the pill?" she teased.

Flustered and in dire need, he shook his head and forced a quick laugh. "No. I. Well. It's been awhile," he admitted. "What I mean..."

"I know what you mean." Her humor fell away when she added, "And I know what I want."

"Are you sure, sweetheart?"

"I've waited so long for this, Daniel, and I don't want to feel anything but you inside me."

His heart swelled, and he understood exactly what they were doing. Making love. Sure he'd had sex before, numerous times, but this was the first time he'd ever made love with anyone. "I've spent the last decade wanting this too," he whispered with effort.

She widened her legs and slid her hands around him. Her fingers trailed down his back, grabbed a fistful of his ass, and squeezed. Hard. A low sexy moan sounded in her throat.

"Please..." she begged.

As sexual energy whipped through his veins, he positioned his cock at her entrance and eased into her, wanting to feel, savor and enjoy every inch as he filled her.

"So good," she whispered and bit down on his shoulder. She bucked forward, forcing him inside. As her cunt swallowed his cock, her scalding heat engulfed him and his throat practically closed over.

Using long sensuous strokes, he began moving, pumping into her, seeking more than just the physical connection. His breathing grew heavy and his balls constricted. As her feminine heat scorched him, tension built inside him, and he knew release was only a push away. Jesus, he needed to slow down, to make this good for her.

"Harder," she cried out, her voice full of want.

"Sweetheart, like I said, it's been a long time for me," he choked out. "If I go harder I just might lose it." Damn he wanted to make her come again before he found release.

"Let's lose it together."

As her intoxicating aroma filled the air, it pushed him over the precipice. Oh what the hell. They could take it slow next time. He pumped harder and rode her furiously, giving her what she wanted. What he needed.

"Yes..." she cried out and squeezed his ass.

Daniel inched back, slipped a hand between their bodies and brushed his thumb over her clit. As soon as his finger connected with her plump nub, she gave a broken gasp and a violent shudder overtook her. As her liquid heat scorched him, her body vibrated and fragmented his last vestige of control. His heart contracted as he gave a moan of surrender.

He drew a shaky breath, gripped her shoulders and stilled, concentrating on the points of pleasure as he filled her with his seed. While he depleted himself, he buried his face in her neck and she held him tight as he rode out the final tremors.

After a long moment, he eased back to see her. She nestled against him and offered him a smile that warmed his heart. Then she gave a contented sigh, stretched and in a teasing voice said, "I believe that just might have been worth the wait."

Daniel laughed out loud. He'd never experienced such emotions with a woman. "Yeah, but let's not wait so long next time."

She arched a brow and ran her fingers over his face, her touch more emotional than physical. "Next time?"

"We've only just begun to test the room, Anna. There's still the bed, the sofa, the tub..."

Anna whacked his ass and his voice broke off. He gripped her hands and braced them over her head. "And of course we need to address this issue of you whacking me all the time."

"What were the consequences again?" she asked, the sex

lilt in her voice hardening his cock again in record time.

Daniel grinned, flipped her over onto her stomach, ran his palm over her lush ass and murmured, "Let me remind you."

Chapter Five

Anna awoke to the sun streaming in through her bedroom window. She stretched and grinned as memories of the previous night came rushing back. Sliding her hand across the bed, she connected with the man who filled her body and heart with warmth.

After their second round of lovemaking, Anna had darted next door to let Candace know she'd be staying the night. When she came back to the room, Daniel had filled the tub with soapy water and the two sipped wine as they indulged in a luxurious soak. Once cleansed and relaxed, Daniel carried her to the bed, where he'd spent the remainder of the night paying homage to every inch of her body. His kisses were so full of emotion and tenderness, there was nothing she could do to shield her heart. Surely to God such affection, compassion and loving concern couldn't be faked, and Daniel wasn't merely trying to finish what he'd been unable to accomplish over a decade ago. Deep in her gut, Anna believed no man would go to such efforts: reading romance novels, spending hours to create a romantic atmosphere, fitting the bed with silk sheets, and even going so far as to fill the tub with scented oils.

Lost in her thoughts, she hadn't realized he'd awoken. "Good morning, Sunshine," he murmured and drew her in for a slow wake-up kiss.

Just hearing his voice had her body stirring to life. "Good morning to you too." As she melted against him, she felt his early-morning arousal. She shimmied and smiled when he gave a tortured moan.

"What's so funny?" he asked.

She was grinning like a fool, but she couldn't seem to help herself. "I'm just happy."

"Me too." He had that strange look on his face again.

"And why are you so happy?" she asked. "Is it because the room worked?"

"Among other things." The grin slowly fell from his face.

She touched his cheeks. "What is it?"

"There is something I've been wanting to ask you for years."

Anna felt her insides tighten. "What?" she asked, rather reluctantly, wanting to put the past behind her and revel in the present for a little while longer.

Without preamble, he got right to the point. "Why did you suddenly stop talking to me?"

Her early-morning bliss began to fade. Now why would he go and dredge up old painful memories and ruin a perfectly good morning? "Daniel—" She made a move to go.

He cupped her elbow and stopped her. "Anna, I really want to know. I also want to know why you didn't invite me to your sweet-sixteen party."

"Because you hurt me," she blurted out, no longer able to hold it in.

The vulnerable look that came over him tightened her heart. "How? How did I hurt you, Anna?"

"I heard you, Daniel."

"Heard me?"

"Yeah, I heard you, Justin Hollis, and the rest of your football buddies talking."

Understanding dawned on his face.

"That's right," she said. "I came over to invite you to my party, but I heard them teasing you about all the girls you'd slept with and asking when you were finally going to nail me, the last on your list." She lowered her head. "Everyone was laughing."

"Christ, Anna." He cupped her head and pulled her to him. He pressed a kiss to her forehead. "I had no idea you heard that. I'm so sorry."

Was he sorry that she'd overheard it, or was he sorry that they'd been discussing her so callously in the first place? She pulled back, but he simply moved with her. "Well I did hear it and there's nothing I can do about it."

"Look, I'm not going to deny that I slept with girls in high school."

"From what I understand you reached out and touched more women than Hallmark."

"No, you're wrong. There haven't been nearly as many as you'd think. Most of my reputation was rumor, because there was only one girl I wanted, and she was the one girl I couldn't seem to have."

She gulped, really wanting to believe that. "Really?"

"Yes, really," he whispered against her cheek. "I never understood what happened between us or why you never invited me to your party. It killed me to watch you dance under the stars with all those other guys."

She dipped her head. "It wasn't the same without you there," she admitted.

Daniel pounded the mattress. "For years I used to lie in bed and dream it was me out there with you."

When his honest eyes met hers and she released those pent-up feelings, old hurts began to fade. "And I used to lie in bed and dream that it was me you were sneaking into your room."

"Really?" he grinned.

"Yeah. It was my secret fantasy."

He gave a rough laugh and cupped her bare sex. "Well, there was a time or two—or a million—that I used to fantasize about you climbing that tree and slipping into bed with me too." He brushed his lips over hers. "Dammit, girl, we've lost so much time."

"What should we do about that?"

"We should try to make up for it." With that his lips crashed over hers. Daniel pulled her beneath him, holding her captive with his body, as if fearing she'd disappear from his grasp. But she had no intention of leaving. She kissed him back with all the love inside her and then spent the rest of the day between the silk sheets with him while he made sweet passionate love to her.

Hours later, Anna made her way downstairs to grab a bite to eat. Daniel had to make a run back to the shop, then to his parents' house. They agreed to meet up later that night at the inn. But Anna had other plans. Feeling naughty and adventurous, she wanted to go back in time, relive their old teenage fantasy, and finish what they'd started in Daniel's room.

Night had fallen as Anna pulled her car into her parents' driveway. Knowing they were down at the Andersons for card night, along with Daniel's parents, she used her key to enter. She quietly made her way through the house and slipped out into the backyard.

That tall tree didn't look quite so challenging tonight, especially since she'd come equipped with loose pants and running shoes. Her heart fluttered as the light in Daniel's room flicked on. Wanting to surprise him, she grabbed a branch and pulled herself up.

As she neared his window, the voices in the room stilled her forward momentum. Damn, he had company. She was about to climb back down, when snippets of the conversation stopped her cold and brought her head around. She glanced into the window to see Daniel with his long-time buddy Justin Hollis—the same guy who'd been harassing Daniel about nailing Anna over a decade ago.

"So that's what the romance novels are all about then," Justin said. "Learning what she likes so you can finally get into her pants." She watched him flip through the dog-eared pages then slap the paperback against his palm. "I got to hand it to you, pal. It was a damn smart move."

When Daniel didn't respond or defend his actions, her heart lodged somewhere in her throat.

"Come on, Daniel, tell me. Did you finally get her to beg for it?" She heard a noise, what sounded like a deep-throated chuckle coming from Daniel. Then he walked across the room to Justin, took the book from his hands and tossed it to the floor, discarded, just like she felt. Used and discarded.

"So did she beg for it?" Justin probed again.

Anna turned her back on the conversation unraveling in front of her as she recalled every moment in Daniel's arms. Oh, Jesus, she had begged for it! Repeatedly. With that sobering reality, her vision went a little fuzzy, and she nearly lost her footing, Anna didn't wait around to hear anymore. She practically slid down the tree, anger rising in her. Angry that she'd thought he'd changed, and angry that she was a fool to think he had.

As tears threatened she bolted through her parents' house, locked up behind herself and spent the next hour driving aimlessly around the town, trying to wrap her mind around the idea that Daniel had used her. That he hadn't changed. That he was that same bad apple from high school.

Even though she'd heard snippets of that awful conversation with her own ears, and her brain warned her to steer clear of him, something in her heart told her no man could fake such emotions. But it was time to stop thinking with her heart, because letting her emotions rule was how she'd found herself in this predicament in the first place.

Deciding to head back to the inn to put the final touches on the room so she'd never have to step foot in the place again, she turned her car around. When she reached the inn, she bolted to the bedroom, determined to get in and out before Daniel arrived.

As she perused the room, her heart pounded against her rib cage. Daniel was right. No woman stood a chance in such a romantic room. She was a prime example. With a lump lodged in her throat, she began to hastily put the pieces together, and that was when Pamina entered, an apple in her hand.

"Anna, what's the rush?"

When she turned to see compassionate green eyes looking at her, something inside Anna gave. Feeling emotionally battered, she dropped to the bed and blurted out the whole damn story. Everything from how she'd loved Daniel in high school to the conversation she'd just overheard.

Pamina brushed Anna's hair behind her ear, then polished her apple on her pretty floral dress. Anna spotted the bruise on the outside skin and was about to stop Pamina from eating it, but it was too late. Pamina bit off a huge chunk.

As Anna looked at the crisp white meat, Pamina tapped Anna's leg. "Just because the skin has an imperfection, a bruise on the outside, doesn't mean that I should just toss it away." Pamina held the apple out for Anna to take a bite, but she declined, having long ago lost her appetite. "You see, Anna. Your Daniel is no different from this apple."

"What do you mean?"

"Sometimes things aren't always as they appear. You thought this apple was bad because it had a mark on its flesh. But after a sampling, it's clear that it's perfectly delicious."

Anna shook her head, unable to think straight. "Pamina—"

"Daniel might not appear so perfect on the outside, but maybe there is more on the inside than you realize." As she sorted through matters, Pamina added, "He's here you know."

Anna sat up straighter and glanced at the door. "I didn't see his van."

"That's because it's parked out back."

"Why?"

"So the supplies were close at hand."

"Supplies? What supplies?" Why would Daniel have supplies? He'd finished the room already.

"He asked me to send you outside." A sparkle lit in Pamina's eye. "Why don't you go see what he's up to?"

With curiosity getting the better of her, she walked to the window to peer out. What she saw nearly stopped her heart.

At least now Daniel finally understood why Anna had cooled on him back in high school. She'd overheard his friends rousing him, but if she'd stuck around longer, she would have heard Daniel shutting them all down. No one talked about Anna like that and got away with it.

Honestly, he had no idea it was *he* who'd hurt her all those years ago, the one who'd shattered her belief in Prince Charming and happily-ever-after. Hadn't he sworn that he'd kick the ass of the guy who'd hurt her? So apparently it was his ass that needed a good swift kick. Not to mention Justin's. Daniel clenched and unclenched his fist, thankful that he'd taken care of that matter earlier.

Her comment about him faking nervousness finally made sense as well. She thought he was putting on a show to get in her pants. Dammit, he hated how that one incident had scarred her so deeply.

Daniel glanced heavenward and took in the black sky and the mosaic of stars glistening overhead. Perfect for what he had planned. He finished fitting the apple tree with lights as he worked to recreate the ambiance from years ago, ever determined to make things right for Anna.

"Daniel—"

He spun around and his heart missed a beat when he saw Anna standing there. God, he'd never met anyone who exuded sweet and sexy at the same time the way she did. A surprised look came over her flushed face as expressive eyes perused the surroundings. She completely took his breath away. Even dressed in loose-fitting pants and running shoes, she had such an innocent sensuality about her. It got to him in ways he couldn't even imagine.

He reached inside his van and flicked on the music from their teenage years. As he held his hand out to her, he felt a rush of love. "Can I have this dance?" he asked, as overwhelming emotions made him shaky. His entire body trembled.

Silence stretched for a long time, then she murmured absently, "My sweet-sixteen party."

He stepped closer, craving the feel of her next to him. "The way it was meant to be."

She gave a rough laugh and he felt a shift in her, a change. "What's the point of this, Daniel?" she asked soberly. "You've already gotten into my pants." There was a hardness in her tone he'd never heard her use before.

He stepped back. Stunned by her words. "I thought you understood—"

She tilted her head and her voice sounded tight. "What I understand is that I'm nothing but a conquest to you. I heard you and Justin earlier."

His stomach knotted. "I'm so sorry. What did you hear?"

"I heard him asking you if you nailed me. Well you did, so congratulations."

He let loose a frustrated growl. "That's it. That's all you heard?"

"That was enough."

"If you'd have stuck around you'd have heard me defend you, and nail him." He rubbed his sore knuckles. "Just like I did over a decade ago. But you didn't stick around long enough to hear it then either."

Anna's eyes widened in utter surprise, and her lashes fluttered. "You punched Justin?"

He rocked awkwardly. "Juvenile, I know, but no one talks about you like that and gets away with it, Anna."

She gave a confused shake of her head. "But I heard you laugh."

He frowned. "Laugh? I hardly think I was laughing."

"Well I heard you make some strange sound. It came from deep in your throat."

"That wasn't a laugh, Anna. That was me trying to keep my

temper in check. Either that or I was going to toss Justin out the window." As a soft tune crooned in the background, he stepped into her and brushed his fingers over her cheek. He stood over her for a long time, just holding her and letting her sort through the turn of events, and praying she believed him. Believed *in* him. As he watched her, he felt something inside her give, and when she softened in his arms, he let out a relieved breath.

"Pamina was right," she said.

"About what?"

"You really are like an apple."

"An apple?" As his heart overflowed with love, and his body filled with desire he drew her closer and they exchanged a long look. "How am I like an apple?"

Anna laughed. "It's a long story."

"And you'll have plenty of time to tell it to me over fine wine and candlelight when we move into the old Murphy place next week."

Her head came back with a start. "The Murphy place?"

"Well technically now it's the 'Long' house, since I bought it for us."

Happiness spread across her face and there was a glint of humor in her eyes when she said, "Pretty presumptuous."

He offered her a crooked grin. "I like to think of it as determined."

"Back in your room, when you talked about us taking possession of our own place...you had this planned from the start, didn't you?"

As her warm familiar scent filled him with need, he lowered his voice and went on to explain, "Don't you see, Anna. I left here long ago because it killed me to be so close to you and not *have* you. When you stopped talking to me, the world as I knew it came crashing down. I moved away, hoping to get over you." He gave a quick shake of his head. "How I thought I could ever get over you, I'll never know. But I'm back now, for good, and I'm determined to make you mine once and for all. I don't just want you in my bed, Anna. I want you in my life. I need you to trust me, to believe in the magic between us, because we belong together."

Blue eyes full of love stared up at him and it nearly unhinged him. "I always thought so too."

As a riot of emotions raced through him, everything inside him reached out to her, and it was all he could do to draw in air. It took effort to speak. He swallowed. "Why are you looking at me like that?"

Her lips twitched, and she moved restlessly against him, conveying her needs. "You have that look on your face again, one I couldn't quite put a name to until now."

"What is it?" he questioned in a soft tone, gripping her hips to pull her against him, harder.

"It's love." Her smile was full of emotion as she flashed dark lashes at him. "It's love, Daniel. And that can't be faked."

He pitched his voice low. "I've always loved you, Anna."

"And I've always loved you."

As his body ached to join with hers, Daniel circled her waist and began to walk backwards, toward the empty van.

"What are you doing?" she asked, her voice a bit giddy.

"About all this time we lost..."

She feigned innocence. "What about it?"

He gestured with a nod over his shoulder. "Do you think...?"

"You want me to have sex in your van?" She whacked him

on the shoulder. "What kind of girl do you think I am?"

Oh he knew exactly what kind of girl she was.

He gripped her hands and pinned them to her sides. "Hey, what did I tell you about hitting me?"

She nibbled her bottom lip, a ruddy hue on her cheeks. "I...uh...forget."

His cock grew another inch as lust surged through him. "Do you need me to remind you?"

Anna's chest heaved with excitement when she said, "I believe I do."

Laughing, Daniel tugged on her hand and pulled her into the van with him where he proceeded to remind her, and to make up for lost time, as he showed her how good they were together, over and over again.

Epilogue

Pamina stood on the sidewalk and glanced at the gorgeous Victorian inn which, after much hard work and dedication by a talented group of professionals, had finally been restored to its former beauty. Everything from the manicured lawn, the repaved walkway to the freshly painted cedar shingles and the fantasy-inspired theme rooms had taken this place from ordinary to extraordinary in a little over a month. Honestly she couldn't have been happier with the end results.

Not only had Lindsay, Candace and Anna created rooms beyond her expectations, they'd all found love in the process—with a little help from her and Abra, of course.

Speaking of Abra...

She glanced down to see him weaving in and out of her legs. Every few seconds he'd glance upward and purr, trying to catch a glimpse of her silk panties, no doubt. Pamina laughed. Goodness, what was she ever going to do with him?

Never missing an opportunity, Abra jumped into her arms, brushed his rough tongue over her cheek. "Oh, I can think of a few things."

Pamina scoffed and rolled her eyes. "I'm sure you can."

Suddenly a dark cloud moved overhead, covering the clear blue sky and chilling the late-afternoon air. A cool gust came out of nowhere, blowing around her body and seeping into

Pamina's bones. Suspecting there was a greater force at work here, she gave a little shiver and pulled Abra in tighter, wrapping her arms around his furry body in an attempt to absorb his heat.

"Pamina," he said, his voice low and sexy. "There are other ways I can warm you, you know. Don't you think it's time you changed me back?"

She grinned. "I suppose it's worth considering. You did manage to help me fill the place with love and passion."

"And don't forget that I saved that romantic moment when Candace and Marc needed condoms." He gave a tip of his head. "Good thing I'm always on active duty."

Pamina laughed out loud. "You weren't on active duty, you were spying. You're nothing but an old tom cat, Abra." She tapped him on the nose.

"I most certainly was not spying," he said, feigning insult. "I was just hanging in the wings in case they needed anything."

She looked into his mystical eyes and smiled. "Well done, Abra. Well done," she murmured and gave him a kiss on the cheek.

Abra purred loudly and shivered in her arms. Pamina reached into her pocket, pulled out a shiny red apple and took a big bite. One minute Abra was snuggled in her arms in feline form, the next his hard muscular body was pressed against hers, chest against chest, groin against groin, his hands holding her tight against his warm flesh.

This time it was Pamina who shivered. And it wasn't from the cold breeze.

Instantly the wind died down, and she had the sneaking suspicion that someone far more powerful than she had cued the frigid breeze to bring them together. She drew in a deep breath and could smell magic in the wind, but it wasn't coming from her or Abra.

She took in the Adonis before her. "Hello, Abe," she said softly, her voice a little unstable as her body turned libidinous.

"Hello, Pamina." He brushed his thumb over her cheek. "Thanks," he said, his voice genuine, his eyes sincere. A moment later, he dipped his head, his mouth so close to hers she was sure he was going to kiss her. Honestly, she would never get used to his charm or blatant masculinity. "And Pamina," he whispered, "You're wrong about me still being a tom cat."

"Ab—"

He cut her off. "I've learned my lessons and now I only have eyes for you." As her insides turned to mush, he gave a slow shake of his head. "I'm just not sure why I'd never seen it before."

She looked deep into his eyes and didn't know what to believe. Truthfully, she'd always loved Abe, loved his spirit, his fun-loving nature, and his zest for life. But how could she be sure of his sincerity. Did she dare hope he'd changed?

As if he'd read her thoughts, he gathered her hand in his. "Come with me."

"Where are we going?" she asked, not sure her rubbery legs could actually carry her up the stairs.

"I have a surprise for you."

Her eyes widened. "You do?"

Abe led her to the staircase until they reached the top level. "Up there."

"In the attic?"

Instead of answering Abe reached out and pulled the cord to lower the stairs. He waved his hand. "After you."

Not knowing what to expect, she tentatively climbed the

stairs. When she reached the top, she stopped and gasped.

Abe came up behind her and wrapped his hands around her waist. "I had the girls secretly design this room for you. I know how much you miss your home when you travel."

"How did you manage? You were a cat."

He grinned and glanced heavenward. "I had help, and believe me, the girls knew there was a whole lot more going on between us."

Her hand went to her chest, "I really don't know how you did it, Abe, but it's beautiful." She waved toward the sky. "It's a replica of my bedroom."

"That's because I want you to feel at home when you come back to visit the girls."

"How did you know I'd come back?" Once a job was done they rarely returned.

"Because you've all grown so close, and these girls are like family to you." He gave a sexy grin the curled her toes. "Imagine how surprised they're going to be when you just hand this place over to them."

"I can't wait to see their faces." She took a moment to glance around the room, which was designed in warm whites, fluffy throw pillows, her favorite rocking chair, and numerous bowls full of ripe apples to add a splash of color. She felt a little teary. "That's the sweetest thing anyone has ever done for me."

"Really?"

"Yeah, really."

He made a tsking sound. "Then you've been hanging out with the wrong people."

"I've been hanging out with you," she teased, trying to lighten the mood.

His voice dropped an octave, to show the seriousness of his

words, she supposed. "Things are going to be different, Pamina. Very, very different, but also very, very good. You have my word on it."

"Your word, huh?"

"That's right." His deep voice seeped under her skin and elicited an erotic shiver. As he looked at her with need and desire, unrequited passion moved through her.

She touched his chest. "What else do I have?" she asked playfully.

He placed his warm hand over hers. "Well, besides my word, you have my heart..." He got quiet for a moment, and then she spotted a wicked gleam in his eyes. "And if you're really, really good, I might let you have my body too."

"Oh, but Abe, I have been really, really good."

He scooped her up. "Well, in that case..."

As heat moved through her Abe laid her out on her cloud-like bed, where he proceeded to remove her clothes and spend the first night of the rest of their eternity offering her his heart and his body.

About the Author

A former government financial officer, Cathryn Fox graduated from university with a bachelor of business degree. Shortly into her career, Cathryn quickly figured out that corporate life wasn't for her. Needing an outlet for her creative energy, she turned in her briefcase and calculator and began writing erotic romance full-time. Cathryn enjoys writing dark paranormals and humorous contemporaries. She lives in eastern Canada with her husband, two kids and chocolate Labrador retriever.

To learn more about Cathryn Fox, please visit www.cathrynfox.com. Send an email to Cathryn@Cathrynfox.com or join her chat group, http://groups.yahoo.com/group/wicked_writers/.

CPSIA information can be obtained at www.ICGtesting.com
Printed in the USA

236702LV00003B/81/P